On Cloudrock the penalty for imperfection is death: death by the long fall into the void, through the poisonous mists and gases that rise from the deadlands far, far below.

The two tribes who survive on the Rock, the tribes of Day and Night, keep their families tight, their bloodlines pure and true, by incest, by cannibalism and by murder. Parcelling out their tiny world in measures of light and time, they wrap themselves in ritual and taboo, each family denying the presence of the other.

THEN CAME THE SHADOW:
born to the matriarch Catrunner, the Shadow is deformed – a neuter dwarf – a natural candidate for instant death. But for this mutant, fate intervenes. The Shadow may live – on the condition that none acknowledge its presence: one word, one glance, and the Shadow will join its luckless kin in the long death-flight.

Surviving on the outskirts of the family, the Shadow's very existence creates an unspoken question that challenges the ties that bind. This is the Shadow's tale . . .

CLOUDROCK

CLOUDROCK

GARRY KILWORTH

UNWIN
PAPERBACKS

LONDON SYDNEY WELLINGTON

First published in paperback in Great Britain by Unwin® Paperbacks,
an imprint of Unwin Hyman Limited, in 1989

© Garry Kilworth, 1988

UNWIN HYMAN LIMITED
15–17 Broadwick Street
London W1V 1FP

Allen & Unwin Australia Pty Ltd
8 Napier Street, North Sydney, NSW 2060, Australia

Allen & Unwin New Zealand Pty Ltd with the Port Nicholson Press
Compusales Building, 75 Ghuznee Street, Wellington, New Zealand

British Library Cataloguing in Publication Data

Kilworth, Garry   1941–
Cloudrock
I. Title
823'.914 [F]

ISBN 0-04-440308-9

Set in Palatino by Computape (Pickering) Ltd
and printed in Great Britain by
Cox & Wyman Ltd, Reading

To the memory of David Islwyn Lewis, priest, humorist, friend, who while in his eighties trounced me more times on his snooker table than I care to remember. This novel was begun the year he died.

The real voyage of discovery consists not in seeking new landscapes, but in having new eyes.

Marcel Proust

CLOUDROCK

Chapter One

All this was a long time ago, when I was a shadow – the shadow of my elder brother, Clay.

Being one of the *unwanted* I was never given a name. It was obvious from my deformities that I was asexual and could never bear or produce children, so they indulged my brother's whim and allowed me to live amongst them, though I am sure my unique position – an *unwanted* among the Family – was considered to be temporary. It was never intended that I should reach adulthood. If the nuisance in me had ever outweighed my usefulness to Clay, then Catrunner, our mother, would have had no hesitation in tossing me from the sacrificial rock to my death. It was only because my mother was a strong personality amongst the Family, and Clay was her favourite, that I had escaped thus far.

I lived from day to day, a touch, a look, away from death. Shadows, though visible, are disregarded. They are unacknowledged. They are the insubstantial phantoms of a physical presence that drift behind their hosts like thin, black ghosts. Shadows are cold, do not have feelings, and melt away in the darkness. I was a shadow in all aspects but one: I did have *feelings*. Sometimes they were so strong they were painful and when I could not be with Clay, I would curl up in my nest in the rocks and nurse my hurt until I fell asleep.

Our village was situated between the forest and the lake. We lived in yurts – or at least, Family members did – made of animal skins: tents, with pliable pole frames. In the caves on the far side of the forest lived the second Family. We met only occasionally, during twilights, for they hunted at night, while we hunted by day.

It was around my eleventh birthday that Flower became pregnant. She was the sister-wife of Reedscar and just eighteen years old. I watched her belly grow larger as she moved around

1

the village, singing to herself in a quiet voice. When she was carrying for five months she had to stay at home, rather than go hunting with her brother-husband and she cried because she wanted to be with him all the time. They had not been married for very long.

Flower was a pretty girl, with long, black hair that reached her waist and she had a soft look to her eyes that endeared her to me. I felt sure that, had I been one of the Family, we would have been good friends. Of course, she never spoke to me or acknowledged my presence, even though she often caught me raking through the ashes of the main fire for scraps of food in the early hours.

Sometimes I would sit and watch her in the sunset, as she stroked the taut skin beneath which was new life, letting the last rays of the sun warm the big, brown swelling. Then her brother-husband would come outside their yurt and place his cheek against her belly and they would both giggle like small children. They seemed happy. Of course, they fought the way all Family did, but the fights were short-lived and not serious.

I watched her all the way into her ninth month.

Just before dawn one morning, she gave birth. I heard the wail reach up into the starless night and then the baby's cry followed closely behind. The two sounds came almost together and I felt my heart quicken as I realized what must happen. The baby was to exchange one darkness for another. From the darkness of the womb it would go immediately to the darkness of the grave.

A group of matrons, attendant at the birth, came out of the yurt followed by a distraught-looking Reedscar. The light of the morning was just seeping through the clouds overhead. The father called a lament in a loud tone, to wake the rest of the Family, and they came sleepily from their yurts to join the procession, which made its way around the lake and across country, towards the edge of the plateau. At the head of the procession was the Greatgrandmother, carrying the newly born babe of Flower and Reedscar. I scurried beside my brother Clay, who looked neither to the right nor left, but kept his eyes fixed on the back of our mother, Catrunner.

We passed the dark shapes of the forest trees in complete silence. There was no need for any talk. One of the Night Family paused in the act of trussing a monkey he had killed. He was

2

standing on the edge of the forest, in which he had been hunting, and watched us pass by. He gave no sign of greeting, nor was any expected. The death of the small creature he held in his hands was strong in my nostrils. The spidery, hairy arms of the monkey dangled loosely and pathetically from the hunter's strong sinewy body as he draped it over his shoulder.

The hunter stared too long at my crooked form and since he was not of our Family I began to get concerned and ran amongst some ferns, to rejoin the group later on the path.

We found a dark stream, sluggish through recent lack of rain, and followed it along until we reached the perimeter. The group stopped. Reedscar stepped forward and took the crying baby from the Greatgrandmother's arms. He walked to the edge of the precipice.

Without further ceremony he grasped the child by one leg and tossed it over the edge of the world.

Small limbs stretched outwards from the tiny body, forming a star in the void. I watched the little white shape plummet down, into the mists of the Deadlands below. It was over. One more *unwanted* had gone to its death. I had seen what had caused it to be treated in such a way. It had been born with misshapen legs.

After the others had left, I stayed on, near the edge and watched the sun rise. Below me I could see the shape of my world in the shadow cast upon the Deadplace below: a mushroom with a thick base to its stem. We lived on the top of this mushroom, which we called Cloudrock, which was forested grasslands forming a huge thick ring around a central lake. It was a place of solid-foam white coral, like cloud gone hard, and when the lake became too full of rainwater it sent out streams of watery legs towards the edge of the plateau. There they formed thin waterfalls that dropped to the Deadlands below.

Because of the overhang, we could not see directly below Cloudrock, but out onto the Deadplace beyond, which was a flat area stretching as far as the eye could see, covered in white sparkling dust that hurt the eyes when the sun's glare struck its crystals. There were always mists down there too: drifting, confused and confusing, rippling their way over the surface of the land of dead spirits. Ghouls and ghosts of the *unwanted* lived down there. Crooked creatures, like me, but without real bodily forms. They were disparate pieces of spiritual flotsam, washed on the winds, wafted by the breezes, to remote corners. They lived in the constant misery of knowing that they could never become one with Redgod, the bloodspirit that streaks the sky at dawn and dusk. Only Family could become part of that ancestral bloodstreak: only the pure-blooded men and women, perfect in body and mind, could die in the knowledge that they would live again as part of the sunrise and sunset. The clustering of the bloodsouls of my ancestors during these times was an awe-inspiring sight but one I would never be part of. They watched over the Family with jealous eyes, ensuring that only the pure would be eaten at death and remain within the circle.

I stared down again. There was nothing below me to mark the fact that the baby had ever existed. There was no hole in the mist, nor was anything disturbed beyond my emotions. The little deformed creature was now amongst its own kind. I turned away and began running back to the village to join my brother in the day's hunting. I passed tall rocks that stood high above the lush vegetation. I loved my home for its rocks. They whispered to me, and though their language was strange we came to understand one another as I grew older, in the way that a man and his dog do. Somehow I knew I was closer to them than anyone else on Cloudrock (Clay excepted) and that made me special. They had energy and power, were dark and mysterious. They were mystics, saturated by time and ancient memories, which filled their every vein and pore. They had souls.

I skirted the freshwater lake. My feet made padding sounds on the shore and I could smell the earth awakening beneath the sun. It was a good smell: fresh and clean. The scent of drying grasses and damp leaves filled my nostrils and I breathed deeply as I ran. I was alive. The warm sun felt good on my small, naked body: burned gently into my brown skin. I could hear the stirrings of the forest creatures as they began their day and the plopping of the fish on the surface of the lake. All around me was life. Parrots were screeching obscenities at one another, the way family members did, and monkeys gossiped at rapid pace like hunters around a fire. A wildcat vacated the path in front of me as it saw me bearing down on it, slinking away into the undergrowth with an air of annoyance at being disturbed. The brightening sun was bringing out the colours and markings of the live world around me and I thrilled to my own existence. *I* was alive.

4

My brother Clay was washing in the lake when I arrived at the village, splashing water over his crouched lean form. My brother was very good to me. He never acknowledged my presence and I lived to anticipate his needs. If he had, just once, called, 'Hey, you!' I would have been thrown the way of my two younger sisters, the way of the child I had seen falling like a stone into the mists that very morning.

He stood up, the water shining on his skin, like a young god. As I approached him he stared vacantly over the top of my head. Clay loved me, I was sure, otherwise he would have spoken to me. He would have acknowledged my presence with knowing eyes. Instead, he ignored me. He must have loved me very much, though perhaps he loved Tilana more. I was with him on that day he met her. He was almost eighteen. She was two months away from the same birthday.

Twilight, and overhead the sky was bloodstreaked, with flecks of black weaving turbulently through the rushing clouds. According to the calendar it was a Good Day. A storm was gathering fast above Cloudrock. I liked to see our ancestors, the bloodspirits in the sky, so angry. It seemed to justify the rage within myself.

Clay was standing on an outcrop of rock, a dark silhouette against the dawn, stroking his bow in thought. I sat, hunched behind some ferns, some few yards away. I was wondering whether we were going to turn back to the village because of the impending storm, or continue the hunt. We could both smell wild pig to the south but I awaited my brother's move.

Finally, he descended from the rock and began a slow jog towards the source of the odour. We were going to hunt.

It was exciting to see Clay run. His dark, lean body moved with such suppleness I could have shouted for joy. Instead, I followed silently behind him, my own shorter legs having difficulty in keeping up with him. As we drew closer to the pigs we slowed the pace, until we were some fifty rods downwind and crawling through the grasses.

There were about seven of them rooting around with their snouts amongst the palm trees. Clay had already fitted an arrow to his bow and we crept forward, the grasses scratching at our bellies and the storm flies sticking to our sweat. I was unable to brush away the insects that entangled themselves in my hair, for

5

fear of scaring away the pigs. The irritation they caused me however, was compensated for by the excitement I felt.

The atmosphere was heavy, bearing down on our naked bodies with a damp weight and I knew that soon the rain would fall in torrents and the visibility would become too poor to see a rod in front.

Clay stopped, and carefully parted the grass at the edge of the clearing. Around us the insects hummed and crackled and kicked up such a din I was sure they were warning the pigs of our approach. Gradually, the bow was slid into the opening Clay had made and he took aim with the weapon horizontal. One of the pigs had its trotters, goat-like, on the base of a trunk and was chewing some berries from a low branch.

I heard the 'thwunk' of the bow releasing the arrow.

Suddenly this pig stood up completely on its hind legs like a human, staggered two paces and gave out a terrible shriek. For one moment I thought it was going to run at us on its hind-quarters, screaming in rage, but then it fell backwards, kicking and squealing. The other pigs scattered, one of them heading straight for our hiding place. It was a young boar and I could see the fear travelling over its face like ripples over water. It kept coming, directly for Clay.

Clay half stood, seemingly mesmerized by its charge. He made no attempt to run or reload the bow and when the boar was some five rods from him I leapt out and ran towards the creature, throwing myself on its back and wrapping my small arms around its head. It kicked and spun in its tracks, snapping with its vicious mouth at thin air. I gripped with my legs around its middle, squeezing hard, until it grunted and quickly rolled over with me, into some thorns. My legs slackened and released the animal which ran back, into the forest.

When I stood up, picking out the painful, long spikes, the boar was gone. Clay was tending the pig he had shot, cracking it over the head with a stone. He deliberately turned his back on me as I approached and so I knew he was pleased with me. His rejection of me was comforting.

We tied the pig's legs together and pushed a pole through them, hoisting it onto our shoulders. The grassland was alive with dancing spots of white and black as the insects heralded the imminent rain. A heavy globule of water hit my shoulder and we started to run, looking for shelter amongst some rocks. As the drops increased to a stream, we found a dark overhang and crawled underneath.

We had only been there a few moments when we heard the sound of running feet mingled with the drumming of the rain. Then heavy breathing like someone gasping for air after a hard swim and choking on water. Suddenly a figure came tumbling in beside us and on seeing the place occupied, crawled away quickly to the far side of the shelter.

The rain roared down. No one said anything for a long time.

In the gloom of our shelter I could see Clay's eyes studying our companion, a young woman. Her own eyes told us she was one of the Night Family: they were large with irises as dark as black pebbles. Chance meetings such as this, with the other Family, were not uncommon at dawn and dusk, though we rarely did more than just acknowledge one another. My brother regarded her for a long while before he finally spoke.

'My name is Clay,' he said.

The girl turned slightly away and let her head drop so that her long black hair fell over her face, obscuring her features. We could no longer see those mushroom eyes and Clay began humming softly to hide his embarrassment. He plucked at his bowstring, pretending to make music to accompany his tune. Then he said abruptly:

'Don't you have a name? Are you mute? Let me see your tongue.'

I heard a sigh that became a whisper, then an audible word. The word was 'Tilana'.

'Tilana. Tilana,' muttered Clay, as if tasting it like a piece of food on his palate. 'Strange names for a strange people.'

Suddenly her head jerked up and there was anger in those round eyes.

'Strange people yourself. Who are you to call us strange people? Who asked you to speak to me? Leave me alone. The storm will be over soon.'

'Funny people,' mused Clay, ignoring the outburst. He seemed amused. 'Hunt by night, not by day. Live in caves, not in yurts.' He twanged the bowstring as if to emphasize a point he had made.

'Leave me alone.'

7

She pulled her knees up to her face, resting her chin on them, and wrapped her arms tightly round her shins. She looked like a tortoise that has lost its shell and does not know where to hide itself.

The rain was a wall of water now and I could hear the whispering rivulets running from the rocks above our heads, forming little waterfalls: imitations of those larger ones that fell from the lip of Cloudrock when the lake overflowed, shooting out into space and dropping as spray onto the Deadlands far below. My nose tickled, as some drips fell from the ceiling of the shelter onto its tip, and I sneezed hard.

Tilana suddenly said, 'Who's that? Your child?'

I squirmed closer to the rockface, trying to merge with the granite, and prayed to Redgod that Clay would not look at me.

'Don't you have a shadow?' he asked her.

'Yes, when the moon shines.'

'Well I have a shadow all the time, even when it's dark like this.'

'I see a person . . .'

'I see a shadow,' snapped Clay.

She stared hard at me, her eyes made for the light of gloomy places such as our shelter. I looked back at her and she seemed startled. Probably by my wonky eye. Then her glance took in my size and obvious age.

'An *unwanted*?' There was surprise in her tone as well there might be. The Night Family customs were the same as our own, since we had all been one family at a time now past.

'A *shadow*,' insisted Clay, becoming angry and I suppose not knowing quite how to handle the situation.

She continued to stare at me and I was terrified she was going to speak directly to me. There was no taboo against speaking to an *unwanted*. It was simply that most of us were killed not long after birth and my situation was one that had arisen out of particular circumstances, *unique* circumstances. There were no rules for such a thing outside my own Family. But she seemed to understand the need to ignore me and began contemplating the rain again.

'How old are you?' asked Clay, suddenly.

'Seventeen – eighteen soon.'

He smiled. 'Me too. We must have been born close together –

in time I mean.' He reached across the space that separated them and touched her cheek before she could withdraw. A hurt expression crossed her face and she said, 'In two months I must marry my brother. He would kill you if you touched me.'

'My mother would kill me first,' he laughed. 'Mother is a very jealous woman. I have no sister, so I must marry Catrunner soon . . .' He began doodling abstractly in the dust, still muttering, 'Catrunner, soon to be my mother-wife. Don't worry. You're safe with me. Oh, yes. The taboo is safe with me.'

Tilana seemed to gain some satisfaction by announcing, 'Soon I will have a brother-husband and will not need to hunt alone any more.'

'By night,' muttered Clay.

'Yes.'

'Under the cold light of the moon, when it's there, instead of bathing in the glorious sunshine. That white skin – there . . .' he touched her again. 'Like a fish belly. The sun would fry you like a fish, crisp and red. Look at me . . .' He showed her a brown arm. 'Don't you wish you had brown skin like mine?'

She grimaced. 'The same colour as dirt,' she sneered.

'Clay,' he corrected. 'Clay isn't dirt. Clay is useful.' He extended his arm again. 'Put your hand in mine,' he commanded.

She hesitated, then reached across, placing her slim white fingers into Clay's palm. There was a moment when they looked at each other with frightened eyes, then Clay said, 'The moon and the sun. I suppose we need them both. You're not really strange.'

'This is wrong – Clay. We mustn't touch. You know.'

'I know. There's no harm in holding hands is there? We can't get babies that way.'

'No, but other things happen. They start and maybe we won't be able to stop them. I don't know. It's better to keep all the laws, even the small ones. Then you can be sure of being right. The Greatgrandmother would . . .'

'It was only a touch – I know. I know. The small ones too.'

Tilana suddenly made as if to leave, though the rain was still falling heavily. Clay said, 'Don't go yet. Stay and talk.'

'I have to go. The sun will be out after the rain and as you have told me – it will burn my skin. I'm already late. I didn't intend to

9

hunt so long in the dawn but I caught nothing last night . . .'
Suddenly there was the mooning note of a horn suspended in the air above the lake.

Day was officially beginning. In my mind's eye I saw the hunter with his or her lips to the instrument, standing on a rock above the lake, calling in the Night Hunters, sending out the Day Hunters. The sound lifted my heart – not because of its message, but for what it was: itself. It filled the hollow sky with its rounded form and I wanted to get up there, on the back of this substantial note, and ride away into the clouds to where no person had ever been before. Such a note! Worthy of a great beast calling to the sun. Worthy of Redgod herself, when pleasure filled her veins.

'You – you can have my pig. Here,' said Clay.

I caught my breath having come down to earth with a jolt. What was he doing? Giving away his kill to a stranger? He was mad.

'There's still a whole day left. I can get another one,' he added, almost pleading with her.

'They wouldn't like it. Your Family. Besides, I hunt with a spear. There's a shaft of an arrow in the pig's chest.'

Clay took hold of the pig and wrenched the wooden arrow from its ribs. Then he put it back again and twisted it round, several times.

'There, the wound is bigger. You can't tell it from a spear thrust now. I *want* you to have it. It's a gift. You can't refuse a present.'

She looked longingly at the carcass. 'It's twelve moons since I took home a pig.' Then she added, 'I can kill pigs you know. I'm as good as you . . .'

'Of course you are. I didn't say you weren't. I just . . . please take the gift?'

She stared at the plump kill again, and then, without another word, took out the carrying pole and began to drag the meat out into the rain. Clay watched her and then jumped up and ran outside. When I followed the rain was easing off and I found him standing on a rock, observing her progress towards the caves where she lived. We studied her white form as she struggled with her load. The rain would help her, letting the carcass slide across the wet surface of the grass. Then she was out of sight, amongst some tall ferns.

'Tilana,' called Clay, through cupped hands.

There was no answer and after a while he returned to the overhang for his bow.

We had lost our pig.

Chance meetings with people of the opposite sex can be expensive as well as dangerous.

Chapter Two

Catrunner, our mother, was waiting at the entrance to Clay's yurt. She was a dark woman, bred for tallness and speed like all the hunters, and her eyes were sharp and penetrating. She had a high forehead caused by continually leaning over a fire and singeing the front of her hair. Her chin was sharp and pointed, like the bill of an axe, and one shoulder dropped lower than the other due to a broken collar bone that had knitted at the wrong angle. Everything about her physique and character had a sharpness to it, like a well-honed knife, yet I knew she could be kind and gentle if in the right mood. Even to me.

Several times, when at peace with herself and the world, she had thrown away a bone with more meat than was frugal sticking to it, knowing that I would pick it up, since I was quicker than the cats and dogs.

Most of the time though, she was as taut as a bowstring and I avoided her as much as possible. It was not that she was physically violent towards me, for that would have meant she acknowledged my presence, but I was afraid of her eyes. They never rested directly on my person, but on some object near me and I could sense her growing disapproval of Clay's unspoken attachment to me. It was obvious that she was jealous of anyone, even a neutered shadow, who spent time with her beloved son.

That evening, the day we had given away a pig, she looked especially agitated and beckoned Clay as we approached. They disappeared into the yurt together and I took the monkey we had killed and placed it with the other game beside the fire. Clay had dropped his bow at the entrance to the yurt and I picked it up and ran my fingers over the magic symbols carved in its stock. Clay's uncle-father had done the designs two seasons before, prior to his death by a fall into a crevice. His craftsmanship had been good – the neat, tight strokes depicting two hunters joined by their hands and feet, so that they arched away from each other,

12

one a female, the other a male. Family. The circle. On the other side of the bow was a female mantis eating her mate. We came from the Family and went back to the Family: from the belly of woman to return to the belly of woman. This was how it was, and it was right. The women ate the remains of the dead.

No one was ever lost from the Family, except those like me – an *unwanted* – and those that could not be retrieved, like my uncle-father. His loss had been mourned for many days but the body had been jammed deep in the chasm, its sides too sheer. He was gone, no longer part of the great circle. Only his work-manship and wooden stool remained. It was a terrible thing when a family member's remains could not be eaten by the women. To be denied access to Redgod's blood-spirit world in the sky was to be denied an afterlife.

I took the bow and placed it by Clay's stool near the central hearth. There were some one-hundred-and-thirty members in the Family, and their sacred stools encircled the camp fire. Farmers, fishers and hunters would soon gather to cook and eat the game. I found some bones amongst the previous day's ashes with a little fatty tissue still clinging to them. I gathered them together for my supper and crept away to my nest in the rocks. There I tore at the hardened flesh, crunching on grey cinders along with nutritious meat, the difference between their textures being almost indiscernible. When I had finished, I gathered some berries and a few nuts to complete the meal. Then I lay in my nest, which was still a little damp and steaming from the day's rain, and fell instantly asleep.

I awoke sometime in the middle of the night. The moon was full and cast a pale light around the forest edge, where my old companions, the shadows, waited patiently for some messiah to rise up amongst them and free them from bondage. Beneath me, in their dark and distant way, the rocks murmured their secrets to one another. I listened to the breeze that ran its fingers through the leaves of the bushes, and to the far call of the waterfalls, full-blooded after the rain. I failed to find comfort in their sounds however, and rose to listen outside Clay's yurt.

The only sound was that of shallow breathing. I went to the back of the dwelling and slipped beneath the skins that were draped loosely over the frame. Clay was asleep near the faintly glowing hearth square and I crawled to him, putting my arms

13

around his hard, muscled chest. He grunted and stirred, then settled again.

In this way I risked death many nights. But I needed the contact, the comfort of another human's presence more than I feared losing my life. Clay drove out the evil spirits, the bad dreams, with his warmth and the purity of his body and soul. Before the dawn's multicoloured face came up over Cloudrock, I would have to be gone.

This was the way it was, and it was right.

Chapter Three

I felt the bite of the axe as surely as if it had been my trunk and not that of the tree which underwent the blows.

The tree had been considered dangerous, being in the middle of the village and a giant in its proportions. When I was younger I used to consider its natural architecture my own world, with its own inhabitants. There were small mammals that burrowed between its roots; insects and beetles made journeys in the valleys of its bark; butterflies, moths, stick insects and other delicate creatures decorated its leaves; there were holes which harboured bright eyes and nests for the less inhibited birds amongst its branches; fruit bats made periodic visits in the twilight and small green frogs, cicadas and lizards sounded in dawn and dusk.

At the very peak of its swaying trunk was the nest of the ruling predator – a sharp-taloned hawk.

A world. A whole world, like Cloudrock. Its creatures must have thought it eternal, invincible. But it came down in a single day. It came down because it was in the way of humankind. I suppose if you have the power and something is in your way, even a whole world, it is tempting to sweep it aside, to destroy it to get what you want?

It was a Neutral Day in the calendar. The horn had not yet sounded. One of the tasks I set myself each morning was the rolling up of Clay's yurt walls, so that a breeze could blow through the tent, dispersing the smell of sleep and caress him gently awake. That morning was no exception. Shortly after I had done my duty Catrunner came to see Clay with her sister-niece, Yellowbark. The two lean, tall women passed me without a glance but I sensed a tension in Catrunner's walk and there was flintiness to her aspect. Was I responsible for that, or some member of the Family? I scuttled behind the yurt to be out of sight and, hopefully, mind.

'Clay,' I heard Catrunner say, 'wake up son. I've brought Yellowbark to instruct you on the marriage – the ceremony. Wake up, come on boy! Quickly.'

I peeked through the gap underneath the rolled skins and saw Clay rise lethargically from his bed. He looked at Yellowbark with a sulk on his face.

'Ceremony? Oh . . . can't you do it, mother? Later? Why does *she* have to come here?'

Catrunner placed a fond hand on his shoulder.

'Because it's not good luck.'

'I don't care about that. I can't stand that woman.'

Clay had never forgiven Yellowbark for a thrashing she had given him as a ten-year-old when he had left a harmless snake in her bed. I remember her screams. They were delightful to me at the time.

Our mother began to get angry.

'You'll do as you're told, child. You're not of age yet. And even when you are, the Family's rules have to be obeyed – you hear? Now,' she pinched his cheek, 'go and wash and come back here quickly.'

He shrugged her other hand from his shoulder and ran out of the yurt and down to the lake. I watched him stand on a rock with the other morning bathers around him. The sunlight was touching the lake delicately below him as he poised for his dive. Then he was gone, leaving barely a ripple on the surface. He came up, thrashed around for a while, then returned to the waiting women.

He shouldered Yellowbark as he passed but she made no attempt to retaliate. This seemed to anger Catrunner. I always knew when she was angry: her nostrils became pinched and white. She gripped Clay's wrist and appeared to be fighting for control of herself. Then she said, 'Pay attention to the talk son. If you want me afterwards, call.'

When she released him I could see red marks where her strong fingers had squeezed his flesh. Our mother left and Clay squatted on his stool opposite Yellowbark.

'The first stage is the vigil,' she said to him. 'You and your mother will paddle out into the lake, far from the shore, in separate canoes. There, on the quiet waters, you will spend the night with Redgod, questioning your life and its purpose and

16

making your vows to uphold the Laws of the Family and its traditions. To promise to show no weakness for an *unwanted* child, no matter how much . . .'

Clay interrupted, 'I understand all that.'

'I hope you do – especially the last part.'

This was an indirect reference to me.

'When the night is over, you should feel purified of bad thoughts – if you do not, then your vigil is incomplete and you must remain until that state enters your spirit. Some time during your vigil you must mingle blood with your mother. She will show you where to cut and bind. When you return to the shore the Family will take you to the feast where Greatgrandmother will cord you to your mother, who will then be your mother-wife. After the feast, there will be the dance of the sacred circle and you and Catrunner may go to the marriage hut, high in the trees, to consummate your union. You are lucky – your mother is an experienced woman. Had you a sister, you would have had to experiment with the ways of love.'

'I am *lucky*,' Clay said, sardonically.

'If you wish,' she continued in a lower tone, 'I can explain the love procedure to you now . . .'

Clay blushed and shook his head violently. 'That's not necessary. We talked amongst the boys – I know what to do.'

'Boys often have false ideas. Perhaps you have some misconceptions . . .'

'No. Leave me alone. Get out of here. I don't want to hear any more.'

'As you wish.' She glared at him and I could see that she was annoyed. She was breathing deeply and red spots appeared on her temples. Clay was the most athletic and clean-limbed of all the youths of his age. He had a beauty that invites trouble. I had no idea what was in Yellowbark's mind but her anger showed she was disturbed for some reason.

She tried again. 'Listen . . .'

'Get out! Get out!' cried Clay.

'Well, if you're sure.'

'I'm sure. I know what to do. Now will you leave me alone?'

I ran away from the tense atmosphere in the yurt. It worried me that she had touched on Clay's compassion towards me. I climbed on the stump of the old tree around which were the three circles of tents, to watch Yellowbark cross to her fisher's yurt on the inner circle. Only the hunters, the élite, were allowed dwellings on the outer ring, away from the smell of stale food and the animal pens.

She passed by me. Then, a few paces on, she stopped and turned towards me slowly. There was a tight smile on her square face.

'Ugly little dwarf,' she muttered.

A chill went through me. She had acknowledged my existence. She had *spoken* to me. No one had heard, but the thing I had dreaded ever since I could comprehend what it meant, had happened. I glanced wildly around me. Where could I go? There was nowhere safe for me now.

I ran to Clay's yurt and lay on the floor beside the sacred hearth. There was no protection for me there, but I felt better when I was near him. I watched my brother purify his hands in the smoke before the day's hunt, but though he must have been aware of my distress, for I was shaking violently, he showed no sign of concern. How could he? From the moment of successfully pleading for my life he had henceforth trained himself to see only a shadow. In order to protect me he had had to erase my true image from his mind and replace it with another, an object he could disregard under all circumstances. For once I wanted him to offer some sign of comfort, to sympathise with me in my terror, but it was not possible. The protective device he had fashioned in his brain formed a wall between us which nothing could penetrate. I was not there in flesh.

The dawn-horn blew in the day.

When we returned from the hunt, in the evening, I watched fearfully for any signs that things had generally changed towards me, but all seemed normal. Yellowbark passed me as I sat by the main fire, but she did not even glance in my direction. It seemed for the moment that she was satisfied with private recognition only. How long that would last I had no way of knowing, but I was beginning to form a plan in my mind, should I have to run from the village and find a hideout. There was an old silk-cotton tree on the far side of the lake which was frequented by wildcats. I determined to fashion a nest in its thick foliage in preparation for the time. Though hunters would not be deterred by mere

18

wildcats, they would not search the tree without good cause any more than they would stick their hands into a hornets' nest.

When the other hunters returned at the end of the dusk-horn's note, I heard that one of them had been accidentally speared. Stone, brother of Catrunner, had received a wound in the thigh. He had been carried back to the village and placed in his tent to await the attentions of the Greatgrandmother.

Night fell quickly. Before the moon rose I saw Clay slip away from the campfire and into the nearby forest. I followed him silently.

The rest of the Family was too busy speculating on Stone and his accident to notice that Clay had gone. I hoped he would be back before the fire died, or Catrunner would wonder where he was. She usually checked his yurt before retiring to her own. I had already guessed his destination and was concerned for his safety.

As I entered the forest I could still hear Stone's loud, distracting curses and self-pitying moans, which I hoped would take Family minds away from the absence of any individuals. Stone had never been one to hide a complaint in his throat and now that he had good cause to attract attention to his sufferings he was making the most of it. I felt sorry for him, but I hated myself for that weakness. I was less than nothing to him and were the situations reversed no thought for me would have crossed his mind for a second. My death cry might make him start, like a cat at the snap of a forest twig, but then he would merely turn his cheek to the wind and wonder would the hunting be bad that day.

As I groped amongst the trees the moon's face came up over the lip of Cloudrock, filling a section of the night sky with its soft light. Shadows sprang from the tall timbers as if they had been locked in the bark and suddenly released. The night creatures began to emerge and I could see the glittering of their large, round eyes. I saw a cat leaping silently from branch to branch, looking for rodents. It passed over me, its tail brushing my shoulder.

After travelling for a short while I came to a clearing. Clay was already halfway across, weaving between the dark rocks, to disappear into the forest on the far side. I was sure now where he was going and the fear in me struggled like a trapped monkey. Beyond that part of the forest lay the caves of the Night Family.

Finally, I caught up with him, just as he was sneaking towards some bushes just below the caves.

The homes of the Night Family were holes peppering the cliff about halfway from its base. They were the holes from which my ancestors emerged when we were all one family, many years ago. They were the holes which protected us from the world when it raged in fire, flood and earth movements. When they became too overcrowded, the one family split into two, the dark and the light. Those that still preferred the darkness of their predecessors remained. The others, my immediate foremothers, were reborn into the day. Children of the moon and children of the sun: we shared a common lineage with each other, reaching back to the first Great Mother and her man, who escaped the fury and died long before their offspring finally re-emerged. Aia and her man were the two brightest streaks of red in the twilights of our lives.

Clay crept slowly to the edge of the clearing before the caves, where the hunters were gathered prior to going out into the forest. I knew who my brother was looking for: the wretched Tilana. She would be the death of both of us, I was sure. Clay had not been able to get her out of his mind since the day they had met under the rockhang and I knew he had been out before this night, following her as she went on her hunt. Some spirit of evil had entered his heart and had turned his face away from his family and towards a forbidden female. I had tried to find some answer from my beloved stones, from the wind and water, but their replies were too deep and dark for my frivolous mind. The answer was in Clay alone and he was too enmeshed to listen to it.

A low murmuring came from the hunting party ahead and suddenly they broke up, heading in different directions from each other. It was then I caught sight of Tilana. Since I was anxious to get back to the village I made a gesture towards her, which Clay followed eagerly. We left, going in the direction taken by her lithe form as she strode out alone.

We stalked her for several rods, walking directly into the face of the moon, until she came to the edge of Cloudrock, where she sat down and stared across at the lunar plains. The great ball of night seemed so close that a floating jump would land me amongst its hills and valleys. I could see vast, dark holes and wide basins full of shining dust. If only it were possible to bridge that distance I would have been free, without a death sentence over my head. How I would have loved to run in that golden dust, kick it up in clouds about myself. That freedom was never to be, though I would eventually reach another kind, but laden with responsibilities.

Clay lay just ahead of me, staring at the silhouette of the Night Hunter against the lunar scape. The sweet smell of the damp grass was in the air and I could hear the distant, joyful rushing of thin waterfalls as they cascaded down onto the Deadworld far below.

Suddenly, Clay called to her.

'Tilana!'

The sound startled the girl and she jumped up, spear in hand, to face the direction of the call. Clay stood up, slowly, revealing his hiding place and as she saw him, she crouched, holding the spear in an aggressive stance.

'It's me. Clay. I want to talk to you again.'

She remained still for a few moments without answering, then, as quick as a cat, she began running along the edge of the plateau. I felt my heart beating faster as I watched, fearful that she would fall. Then, to my relief she struck out inland. It's true that if she had slipped Clay might have been better off, but I did not wish for the death of any person. I gave a sigh of relief mixed with despair and Clay turned. When he realized it was just his shadow behind him, he swung back again and stared at the place where she had been sitting. He went to it and began searching there, as if looking for something she might have left behind. After a while he gave up and made a futile gesture to the moon before setting off, back to the village. I followed, naturally.

The fire was just beginning to die when we slipped between the yurts to join the rest of the Family. There was a deep, red glow to its heart and the cooking had commenced. Clay took his place next to our mother and I sat on the rock within listening distance, out of the direct line of sight of Yellowbark.

On the other side of Catrunner sat Stone. He was Catrunner's younger brother. His thigh was strapped and bandaged: the result of his accidental wound.

I wondered who had been responsible. I had heard that a

21

group of hunters had been stalking a pig separately, had come upon it together and naturally all wanted it and claimed it as their kill. In the general mêlée a spear had found Stone's leg. No one had claimed ownership of the shaft, nor would they now. Catrunner had been one of the hunters in that group. So had Yellowbark. But there had been five altogether and the spears were taken from the rack in the central area every morning. Unlike bows they were public property and had no markings. I felt sure someone was working out a grievance, since accidents of that kind were usually due to inexperience and all five hunters were in their thirties.

I studied Stone's face in the firelight from my perch. He was obviously in pain and picked at his meat without interest, glaring from time to time around the circle.

Such a tangled knot the Family made, full of internal jealousies, suspicions, hatreds – for once I was glad I was not a close part of it all. Who could untie those ugly emotional conspiracies, bound tightly together in blood and marriage? A scarlet knot of tight threads. This was the Family, this band of people – physically beautiful but spiritually ugly. For as long as I could remember they had been picking at each other: goading, baiting, niggling and occasionally flaring into open abuse and violence.

I wondered whether the Night Family were the same way. Whether the members of their Family were as highly strung, as sensitive, as waspish as our own. I was sure they must have been, for we were like two sides of the same nest of vines. The hunters were the worst. Their nerves were as taut as hamstrings. They snapped and snarled their way through life like sick dogs. They lashed out without warning when annoyed. They flew into rages at the least provocation. Even Clay, who was of a calmer temperament than most, was far from placid. He had had his share of clawing fights and bitter feuds.

I studied again the sullen looks of Stone and considered the accident. How had he managed to get between the pig and the javelin thrower? As I stared at him he winced, rubbing his groin, high above the wound. The shadows from the fire intensified the expression of pain on his face. An idea came into my mind as I watched his movements: a suspicion that needed verification.

I crept away from my perch and made my way to the rack of spears. It was dark there, the lamps not yet having been lit, but I groped around taking out the spears one by one, sniffing their points. Finally I came across one that smelled strongly of soap bark. It had been washed thoroughly. Why? It was my guess that the user had scrubbed it to get rid of the lethal thorntree poison on its tip. Stone had an irritation in his groin. If I was correct a deadly red line was travelling up his artery towards his heart. He was going to die. The killer would call it blood-poisoning.

What a tense, intricate family nervework, with its tight defences against all but itself! I was not part of it, part of them, therefore my danger was from the whole. I was like the wild beast, the useless domestic animal or the tree that just happened to be in the way.

Chapter Four

Catrunner was Stone's attacker. I heard Stone, in his delirium, shouting something about the fact that she had once promised to marry him and that Clay should be made to wait for a sister from that union. Shortly afterwards Catrunner went into the yurt where Stone lay sick and he became silent. No doubt the result of some administered drug.

Later the Greatgrandmother said, 'The boy has poison in his blood.'

'It's those spears,' Catrunner replied. 'The dirty blood of the previous kill is never washed from them. Stone's blood has been infected by some filthy creature . . .'

For once, I agreed with my mother, though I doubt she would have appreciated the irony.

Chapter Five

What a day that was!

It was a day when death came out of the sky and went rushing up the nostrils of the Family. Cloudrock was raped, ravished, despoiled, deflowered, by a mighty, thrusting conquerer and I am ashamed to say I found it delightful. It began peacefully enough. These things always do.

Everyone and everything in the yurt had its proper place. There was a side where the women sat and a side for the men. This was not because the men were considered inferior but in order that the main exchange of conversation should be between, rather than within, the sexes.

There was a 'place of honour' – a spot by the hearth, away from the draught, which was used for important members of the Family, like the Greatgrandmother. The young and sometimes animal newborn sat close to the door which faced east. Ropes and weapons were placed at the west end; kitchen tools at the north.

The yurt was the universe in small.

The roof was the sky and the hole in the ceiling represented the sun, both a source of light and an exit point for the smoke. The hearth was the sacred area – the square of the earth – and consisted of the five basic elements of the Family: soil, wood, fire, metal, water. There was earth on the floor, wood in the frame enclosing the hearth, fire within the hearth, metal in the grate and water in the pot on the grate.

Our yurts were dome shaped – constructed of flexible poles that met in a crown at the centre and tied to stakes driven into the ground. Doors were of solid wood and carved with magic symbols. The framework was draped with animal hides and palm mats provided floor covering. To lose one's yurt, in an accident such as a fire, was a disgrace, and the day following Stone's wounding, the whole Family had their yurts destroyed.

The most sacred piece of furniture in the yurt was the personal stool of the occupant – or stools, if there were more than one – which was crescent shaped, cut from a hollowed tree trunk. When the owner died the stool was stained black with berry juice and nailed to a giant log thicker than the height of two men.

The stools of dead ancestors were only approached on bended knees and great reverence was displayed towards them, for the spirits of their former owners came down from Redgod's sky to occupy them from time to time, and one never knew when they were present.

It was Greatgrandmother's job to teach the young about their ancestors and the spiritual world they inhabited after death. A man or woman – or indeed, child – whose body had been consumed by the Family matriarchs, could expect their spirit to ascend to the blood-streaked sky above, where it would be free to roam with its kin. Occasionally it would descend to earth to occupy its stool.

Every child knew that evenings and mornings were the times when the blood-spirits of dead Family members gathered overhead to discuss the business of immortals and watch over Family activities, for these were the times when the crimson was strong.

Even at that young age I was not so much sceptical as impressed by the concept of the birth–death cycle, but one or two aspects of it bothered me. For instance, if members were retained within the circle after death, by ingestion, then by that time we must have absorbed several hundred pigs, innumerable birds and fishes, monkeys, and other fare, into our group. We could count hogs amongst our relations. And, of course, the animals that *we* ate, had already eaten other things themselves. My half-brothers and sisters were therefore worms, or caterpillars; my cousins were tree-grubs and maggots; my aunt was a gnat and my uncle a larva – for their blood had been introduced into the Family since the first mouth that ever took food.

Then there was the fodder to consider.

I should have to count among my foreparents, the blades of grass and leaves of trees that surrounded us. Finally, when I considered the worm, that seems to be eating the very earth itself, I realized that my blood was thickened by mud and dirt, which, having been introduced into the Family before and during the life of Catrunner, I could properly call mother and father.

When I arose that morning the sky had taken on a strange hue – a magenta streaked with black like the quick-feathered strokes of a tailbrush artist. There was a deep, expectant silence too, which made the emerging Family members pause and look about them uncertainly. Something unusual was about to occur but they were unable to define the cause. It was as if some maniac had been busy during the night, strangling all the forest creatures so that not a single life remained. No birds sang; no mammals called to each other from hidden places; crickets and cicadas had ceased their orchestral accompaniment to the frogs.

All was wrapped in the hush of a still morning.

Only the distant hiss of waterfalls, normally drowned beneath the wildlife chorus, provided any background sound. Only one had to hold one's breath to appreciate the mechanical motions of the universe; to eavesdrop on the stars as they swam through space, or listen to moondust stirring in ancient bowls. Men and women talked in whispers, as if to shout were a profanity which would call down holy wrath on the offender.

I stood on my rock and looked about me in wonder. People were afraid. I wanted to run and jump, dance about in glee, for here was something mightier than the Family. Here was some unknown entity that was destroying their smugness, if only for a short time. I wanted to laugh and prance about in their midst because they were afraid, and I was not. I wanted to show them how weak they were, while I was strong – strong in instinct, sharp in memory, for I remembered an old story which the Greatgramma once told, about the mighty bubble of silence that descended on the world before a great wave of water and fire engulfed it.

They were all going to die!

I was going to die too, of course, and Clay, but that was a small price to pay for absolute revenge. All those babies the Family had tossed from the edge of Cloudrock: the spurned, wretched *unwanted* with their weak, watery eyes and twisted limbs; with their parakeet minds and fishlike floppings; with their mewling mouths and terror-fixed expressions – they would be laughing too! They would be splitting those happy idiot faces with red-crescent grins, their tongues hanging muscle-loose between their lips in joy. This was the end of the world, I thought – ha! ha! ha! – and the Family was tip-toeing about in dread, like dark

27

spirits walking on sacred cloud, while I was a happy witness to their destruction.

'The wind is coming,' called the Greatgrandmother. 'We must batten down the yurts as quickly as we can.'

Wind? I thought, disappointed. There was rapid movement in the village now, as Greatgramma's words were absorbed and transformed into activity. Wind? Perhaps she was mistaken? Perhaps this was to be Redgod's last big joke, making the foolish Family run around carrying out useless tasks as her wrath fell upon their impotent, ignorant lives?

But then I felt a light touch on my cheek and heard a stirring amongst the leaves of the bushes. The Greatgramma was right. It was just a wind.

I went to help Clay with his yurt, taking ropes and crossing them over the top, then fastening them to the stakes he was driving deep into the ground. People were using huge rocks as weights on the piles of skins they had taken from the roof and walls, so that the wind could blow through the exposed framework. Domestic animals were tethered to trees and tame birds set free, to be recaptured afterwards. Canoes were strapped to standing stones, their bottoms facing the direction of the wind, and fires were doused to prevent the flames from spreading.

As we worked the strength of the wind increased, until the saplings were beginning to bend to the earth and a mighty creaking and groaning came from the forest, as all the spirits of the trees complained loudly at being woken from a long sleep. Dust and grit began to fly into our faces as we worked. Perhaps the world was coming to an end after all, I thought hopefully.

The Family sat round in a circle, holding hands and praying to Redgod in loud chants. This act on the part of the puny humans seemed to increase the wind's fury. It now screamed through rock crevices in a high voice and began stripping the trees of their leaves. Loud cracking sounds were heard as branches broke. One of the Family was stunned when a flying log struck him on the base of the skull.

The Greatgrandmother rallied us with the shout, 'The caves! We must go to the caves!'

'The caves!' echoed the Family, and they turned their faces into the brunt of the wind, their cheeks distorted and their eyes deep in their skulls. I followed. The caves were those from which we

28

had all emerged long ago, now still occupied by the Night Family. There was an unwritten law which said that in a time of great danger, the Night Family would share their homes with us, but it had been a long time since this had been put to the test. They might have conveniently forgotten such a promise. There was not one amongst us, I am sure, who was confident of a welcome.

It had been so long since any of us had even conversed with the cave dwellers, except by accident, such as in the case of Clay and Tilana. Perhaps they would greet us with a shower of spears and withdraw their rope ladders, leaving us helpless at the foot of the cliff?

As we made our way through the forest, two women carrying Stone on a hide stretcher between them, the tops of the trees began snapping and flashing through the air like javelins. Loose branches battered and crashed their way between tree trunks, drumming out a discordant cannonade around us. On emerging on the far side, a baby was torn from its mother's arms and dashed against a tree, killing it instantly. I myself was lifted and thrown along the ground and had to dig my long fingers into the earth to stop my rolling motion.

We laboured on, the grieving mother's cries adding to the terrible noise of the wind. My own breath was forced down my throat and my long hair lashed at my shoulders like a dozen whips, but the strangeness of the situation excited me. Here was a day quite unlike any other and the Family had been reduced to the level of endangered beasts, fighting for survival. It was a day to remember, to nurture in my breast during the lonely hours, when all slept and I was an outcast in my nest amongst the rocks. At such times in the future, when I was feeling particularly aggrieved or even just reckless, there would be the temptation to run through the village, rousing complacent forms, shouting, 'The wind is coming! The wind is coming!' with the prospect of watching them stumble from their yurts, terror in their hearts and eyes. I bent my body into the wind's force as I considered this marvellous trick, my chuckle lost in its shrill wailing.

By the time we reached the caves hardly anyone could keep their feet for more than a few moments at a time. The rope ladders were lowered without hesitation, weighted by stones, and the climbing began. One man was torn from the ladder twice and thrown into the bushes both times. The loose ropes snaked and lashed at the air and people ran this way and that to avoid being struck by the rock weights. In the general confusion I managed to cling to Clay's back as he ascended like a sure-footed monkey and we entered the darkness of a narrow-mouthed cave.

Deep inside, dim candles were floating in saucers of wax and it took some time to adjust to the light. Eventually I could make out the shapes of people lining one wall of the cave.

There were seats cut into the rock of the cave walls and equipment stacked in alcoves and corners. Right at the far end was a hearth and a pot, but the fire beneath had all but died. The Night Family had ranged themselves along one wall, leaving the other for us. Children were tucked between the knees of adults or were in the arms of parents. The roof of the cave dripped with precious metal spearheads and knives, hanging out of reach of the young and performing their secondary function as ornaments. A fishing net had been rolled into a bolster, which people were using as a footstool. One or two dogs lay flat on the floor, their eyes flickering warily over the faces of the strangers. A tame piglet snorted away in a corner, seemingly unconcerned by the commotion. No one spoke, not a greeting nor a hostile word.

Outside, the wind blew a howling note along the cave entrance that would drown the noise of a colony of parrots. I curled up in a corner and nursed the feeling of satisfaction that I felt at seeing my Family humiliated, having to seek favours from the night people. I was sorry about the death of the baby, in the forest. There were many I wished to see die, but this one small individual death, the death of an innocent, was a tragedy. One little life snuffed out like a wick, filled me with sorrow – genocide only would have been a joy. The Family as a whole I could regard as a malignant entity but I could not despise certain of its individual members. I did not even hate Catrunner, for she was my mother. I *feared* her – almost as much as I knew she loathed me, the ugly issue of her womb on permanent display – but I did not hate her.

What did give me satisfaction was that the wind had robbed her of her identity and personality – she had been just another nameless human being struggling against something far more powerful than herself. The strength of her voice, her gestures, her penetrating eyes, her will – these had been stripped from her like the leaves from the trees, leaving her naked and impotent. She had become unrecognizable from her fellow sufferers, of which I had been one. She had been transformed into an *unwanted* for a short period of time: unwanted by nature and the elements that had the last word on fear and destruction. Her soul had been laid waste and it was good, very good, to know she had joined the *unwanted* in our corner of the world, with all its miserable afflictions, if only for a short while. It was good to know she had experienced rejection. It was good to know she had become *me* for a moment, robbed of the protection of the Family circle; an outsider among outsiders; an outcast from her safe tight knot of brothers, sisters, husbands and cousins, with all the cross-threaded relationships that bound them together.

Her blood was of no use to her in the wind.

Her tall, muscled body a hindrance, not an asset.

Oh, it was good to lock that knowledge in my heart and play with its implications when I wished to hit back. Imperfect Catrunner, you were met in me at last!

The wicks sputtered in their bowls of oil and wax, and shadows slid back and forth along the walls of the cave. Here were my friends of day and night, performing dances behind their hosts; aping sudden movements; turning their actions into a phantom mime.

I grinned for my friends, grinned with them, as they played their silent jokes on flesh-and-blood counterparts; advancing, retreating, in a dumb show of mockery; mimicking them behind their backs. Oh, you funny dark people! Thin race of the walls and floor. How I wish I could be as you – evident, yet inconspicuous; seen but unseen; there but not there. Why didn't the hosts scream at them in exasperation? Snarl at the mockery? Yet here they were, unaware of the silent jeers, the copycat motions, their silly ignorance making the situation a delight to watch: their cleverness, their physical prowess, reduced to foolishness by simultaneous imitation of their gestures. Who can make a grand gesture when the sweep of the arm is duplicated instantly by a dark caricature behind his back? Who can call serious attention to her words and emphatic hands, while a distorted creature follows the motions to exactitude?

As the night people talked in low voices amongst themselves, and my Family likewise, I could see Clay scanning the faces of the women, looking for Tilana. I was suddenly afraid for him. He looked anxious and seemed to lack all vitality, save for his eyes, which burned with a terrible intensity. He was like one of the goats we bred for their blood, draining a little each day from a vein, to mix with milk curdled by urine for our breakfast food. These creatures became listless and apathetic, except for their eyes which burned like lamps, as if all the life-force in their bodies were concentrated in those organs alone. Clay's eyes held that same feverish energy – that high-yellow burning.

I wanted to whisper, *The taboo*! But it was impossible. I was powerless because I was only a shadow. No matter how much I loved him, I could not help him. After that time in the storm, when he had first met her, I tried at night to let the warnings flow from my body, through my arms that held him so tightly, into his hard body – to make him understand that he was destroying himself. The Family would crush him like a beetle. He knew this, yet still his eyes blazed for sight of her and it was a wonder to me that no one else noticed this wild, ungovernable emotion that he was attempting to share with an outsider. His lack of control was all too evident to me and it was surely only a matter of time before others became aware of it too?

'Clay? What's the matter?' Sharp, hard words.

It was Catrunner. *She had found him out.* I wanted to evaporate, join that wind that raged by the mouth of the cave. Then again, I wished I could suddenly transform myself into a monster, to call her attention away from her son, get her to concentrate on something other than his eyes. Both these desires were in me at one time, the former borne of fear, the latter of concern for my brother's life.

'Nothing. Nothing, mother.' But he blushed, caught in the thought if not the deed.

Her voice was low and even.

'Why are you staring like that? Is that the way to return hospitality? They're our hosts. Remember? There's such a hate in your eyes.' Her tone changed. 'I know how you feel, but don't show it. Today we need them and we must be civil. Keep such feelings to yourself until we're out of their homes. We must make a show of gratitude.'

32

In her ignorance she had mistaken love for hate, these two emotions being as close as identical twins.

Her shadow grew fat and ominous behind her, as she was caught in the light of two candles. Even her shadow had a shadow – a wasted creature called up from a place beyond the beyond, woken to give support to its host and confirm the urgent movements with its vague ghosting.

'I wasn't ... I didn't think. I'm sorry. I was just looking. I didn't mean anything.'

Her angular movements became softer but her words were just as brittle as before.

'I understand how you feel, but it's important not to display such feelings. Keep them to yourself. We mustn't quarrel with them – not today.'

'No, of course not, mother. I'll try to – I'll try *not* to ...'

She nodded and seemed satisfied. Clay sank back against the wall of the cave. A huge, shuddering sigh escaped, involuntarily, from his lips. Then he looked about him, nervously, in case someone had noticed. Whether it had been a sigh of relief, or of anguish because he had not found the person he was looking for, I had no idea. My soul cried for him. I could not even pray to Redgod, that manifestation, the scarlet flush which spreads across the twilight sky. For She was the shadow of our blood, the phantom of our life-force, and She was for Family, not for sin. All the blood shadows of our ancestors were in her face and they would call for the destruction of anyone breaking the taboo.

Stone began muttering deliriously and rolling from side to side on his stretcher. I could see the globules of sweat glistening on his face and his eyes looked yellow and vacant in the candlelight. Once or twice he grunted like a pig, startling those around him. No one moved to give him any assistance until, eventually, one of the Night Family women went to the water skins and brought one to him. She washed his face and gave him something to drink. Catrunner then rose and walked casually to the back of the cave, took a drink and resumed her seat. One by one the Day Family followed her example. Some of the tension went out of the air.

Tilana was not in the cave and the disappointment clearly registered on Clay's face, though I was the only one who recognized it as such. I was extremely relieved, for his mood was reckless and I felt sure if she had been there he would have immediately engaged her in conversation and we would have been lost.

Amongst the Night Family was a small, skinny creature of advanced age who wore parrot's feathers around her neck, ankles, wrists and waist. She was Nithma, their Great-grandmother, and the whole night long her huge eyes took in every movement made by any of the Day Family. She herself seemed incapable of motion, as if carved from wood, and squatted in a corner, so still that I began to wonder if her joints had dried and she was indeed on her way to becoming the withered driftroot she seemed to be. Unlike the rest of her kin, her skin was not white but a fungus grey, covered in dark blotches. She looked emaciated, brittle, diseased, and she filled me with terror: a husk of a human being that revealed life only through the rheumy eyes that seemed to swallow me whole whenever they rested on me. Had one of her Family casually snapped off a thin arm and thrown it on a fire like a twig, it would not have surprised me. Her constant appraisal of us was frightening: the toothless puckered mouth, condemning. I would see that gaze in every knotted, gnarled stump in the forest for weeks to follow. She was the goddess of dried death: dust and ashes moulded into form.

I stayed close to the mouth of the cave and listened to the wind screaming at the sky. All natural things have voices which speak to one another – but to understand you must be one of them. Fire talked in short, crackling phrases: complaints I imagined, about being held prisoner and how it would like to break out and run free over the grass and amongst the trees. I was sure that the other elements found it difficult to communicate with fire. It was truculent and moody and often retreated into itself, being more introverted and eccentric than its fellows.

I could not speak to the elements but I could, if I concentrated, guess what passed between them. Water, contrary to fire, would speak to anything that cared to listen. It was garrulous and euphoric and had none of the spite and venom of a spluttering, spitting fire. It bubbled and splashed its empty messages to the earth, air and metal. It whispered to the pebbles on the shores of the lake and sometimes roared to the rock in time of flood.

All the elements could kill.

34

Earth did not speak often but when it did it was a terrible sound to hear. It boomed with the voice of hills or bellowed from the depths of caverns.

Metal, the least talkative, had the most musical voice. It rang out its song in clear, high tones and there was little difference between a song of life or a chant of death.

Water was the most powerful of the five elements. I have heard the snarling and hissing of a vicious fire when it was in an argumentative mood, frightening everything around it with its high temper and ready to flare into violence at the least provocation. I have heard this, yet, when such a fire was threatened by water, placid and gentle water, it was almost immediately subdued. Water had a mighty strength and weight which it would use if it had to, to smother any offending element – displacing air, corroding and destroying metal, washing away the earth and dousing fire. Nothing could withstand water once it was aroused. It was a gentle giant that could crush with its great form and though the earth had as much bulk, it did not have the fluid grace, the easy movement of water. The earth was unco-ordinated and chaotic in its attacks, like a sleeping beast aroused, that strikes out with a wild paw and then settles to rest again.

But then I was listening to the wind, which destroys with its breath, with the very act of speech. The earth had annoyed the air by being so docile and the air was enraged by its companion's lack of interest. Just as one human will eventually become exasperated by the inactivity and passive attitude of another, the wind was lashing out at the earth. Fury. Temper. The wind was screaming oaths at the earth, trying to whip it into some kind of response, while the great beast lay dormant and unmoved. The earth will not be moved if it has no mind to be: it just lies there and takes the punishment, accepting the blows with the amused tranquillity of a father being punched by an enraged infant.

Just before dawn there was a confrontation. One of the night people, possibly terrified by the noise of the wind, ran to the entrance of the cave. Clay, thinking the man was half-crazed and preparing to jump, grabbed hold of him. The Night Hunter struck out and then reached for a weapon on the wall. Catrunner felled him with a blow to the nape of the neck.

Complete chaos ensued. People were screaming, knocking

35

over lamps in order to get out of the way of others, who were lashing out wildly at one another. Yellowbark was screeching at a night youth, raking his face with her long nails. Clay held off a woman wielding a pot of boiling honey and narrowly escaped a scalding.

In the middle of it all, the old woman, Nithma, was shrieking for order. One by one she struck at her own people with a large metal ladle until they had ceased fighting. Finally, only one person seemed unaware that all was quiet: Clay. He was still running up and down at the entrance of the cave, making threatening gestures, as if he had a spear in his hand. His eyes were wild and clearly his mind had gone for a moment. His mother took hold of him from behind, an arm around his throat, and stroked his hair until he stopped struggling and a calmness came over him.

Shortly afterwards, the wind died down.

Chapter Six

It was a Neutral Day in the calendar.

When we emerged from the caves hardly a tree was standing. The whole world had been flattened by a giant hand. I could see as far as the lake, shining like newly polished metal in the distance. I could see where the rivers grew from it – the legs of a squashed silver beetle. All around the lake the land had been flattened: trees, bushes, once-tall grasses, lay close to the earth, all running in one direction: a kind of curving sweep to the south.

The edge of Cloudrock glistened with white, exposed coral in the sunlight, bright enough to hurt eyes that had become too accustomed to the dark of the last twenty-four hours. I blinked away the tears. One of my eyes stared permanently at the tip of my nose and this one gave the most trouble.

The wind had gone, taking with it the last wisp of its tail. All was still and silent. And dead. We were going to have to work hard to feed ourselves over the next few months. There was no place to retreat to. Cloudrock was all the world to us. All. If there had been somewhere else my ugly form would have had somewhere to hide from death. We, the *unwanted*, were life too, after all. In us a heart-beat, a mind whirred with real thoughts; blood carried passion, fear, love, hate and envy through the channels of our limbs. Even a tree, with its green blood and woody heart was given more respect than we were accorded.

The Family made its way down the rope ladders and descended into the horizontal forest. Yellowbark and Catrunner were shouting orders to the numbed group, saying that we would have to skirt the forest and find a path along the bank of a river back to the village. The forest itself was impassable now, with great jagged stumps and huge logs barring the way. Here and there were whole trees torn from the soft earth, the dirty undersides of their grey roots revealed obscenely to our gaze, as if their nether regions had been turned to our faces in an

37

insulting gesture of contempt. Broken limbs lay scattered over the ground in a tangle of wood and leaves. No beasts or birds were to be seen and I wondered if they had left us forever: carried far away on the back of the wind.

At Catrunner's orders the children were lifted onto the shoulders of the adults and I clung to Clay's back as he picked his way amongst the debris. Once or twice he stopped to shift my weight, readjust his burden, but not in an obvious fashion. No one paid much attention to me anyway: each was lost in her and his own disconsolate thoughts, contemplating a bleak near future of hard work and fish suppers. Survival was paramount in their minds – they had no spare consideration for such as me.

'When we get back,' Catrunner was saying to Yellowbark, 'I'll attend to the yurts – you take some of the Family to see if the canoes are still tethered. We'll need the canoes.'

'What about the livestock? Shouldn't we send out search parties?'

'Later. I haven't much hope for them but at least we can eat meat for a couple of days and try to smoke as much as we can before it goes rotten.'

'You think they'll be dead?'

'I'm sure of it. So would we be if we hadn't reached the caves. Much as I hate to say so, we owe the Night Family a favour. And who knows – the wind may come back again? We ought to send them a gift.'

'What?'

'I don't know at the moment. Perhaps one or two canoes. There's plenty of bark around. We'll send two of the young men later, to ask them what they want. Clay and Moss could go.'

The woman who had lost the child the day before was grieving, but her father-husband, a fisherman, was stroking her back and making noises of consolation. At that moment I felt sorry for her, but later I could not help thinking that had the child been an *unwanted* she would have turned her back on it without another thought. Where was her pity for her other unfortunate children? Where was her compassion for her crippled babies? Filial love had a selfishness at its core. She was crying for herself, not her child.

I realized I was becoming heavy, for Clay was muttering under his breath.

'I am strong as the teak, hard like the teak, tall like the teak, tough like the teak . . .' It was the traditional chant of the hunter under duress, but I could not help thinking that the symbol was hardly apt any more. My new image of a teak was that of something laying flat on its back. An unseen force had snapped the teaks like twigs. I slipped from Clay's back and began walking by myself.

So, we had passed the night in relative safety and were on our way back to the village again. The paths had been demolished but of course we knew our environment so well, there was little chance of getting lost. On the left, a daytime moon touched the sky with its pale presence, watching our progress.

'We'll stop by the next stream,' said Catrunner, and the stretcher bearers gave out an audible sigh of relief. Stone was heavy and restless, so that he shifted the load constantly, making their work that much more difficult.

Clay was moody and disconsolate, and frequently looked back towards the caves from which we had emerged. I hoped his obsession with the Night Family was not as obvious to the others as it was to me. One of his young cousins was trying to engage him in conversation.

'These night people,' she said. 'Their hunters were not as tall as ours – not like you or me.'

'How would you know?' snapped Clay. 'It was too dim in there to tell.'

'I only thought . . .'

'People *think* too much. They also *talk* too much. It's doing things that counts. Did they look hungry? Were they short of meat? A hunter's skill is in the results of the work. They seemed to be fine to me.'

The cousin was both surprised and a little crushed by the reply.

She said, 'Well, I suppose . . . I only . . .'

'I know what you suppose,' continued Clay, with the same amount of acid in his voice. 'You suppose that everything we do is *right*, and everything they do is *wrong*. Well, I know one of their hunters and she's as good as you – better.'

The cousin stumbled away from him, obviously bemused by the response she had received to a simple comparison between families. She would be wondering what she had said to Clay recently that had angered him. She would be thinking that there was little doubt that Clay was merely arguing for the sake of it. After all, no one could be considered above one's own Family. It was ridiculous to think that the Night Family hunters were even equal to ours, let alone *better*.

We passed a hillock on which torn stumps of the wounded forest stood in mute testimony to the violence of the storm. Finally we came to the stream and sat down to rest. The sparkling waters jumped and danced around the rocks, calling to me to come to them, but I was conscious of having to remain as much out of sight as possible. As we rested on the grass, Stone began to rave, becoming more delirious by the moment.

'Redgod comes for me!' he screeched. 'Listen! Listen! I hear Her voice. She knows. She knows who did this to me. She will avenge me – you hear Her? Death is in her voice . . .'

We all listened, but the world was calm, save for the bubbling rill and a distant, misty sound of water falling out into the void at the edge of the world.

Suddenly, Stone's eyes opened very wide and he gripped Catrunner's wrist with his left hand. I could see her wincing and I knew it was a death grip that had locked on her arm. Stone raised himself slowly from his stretcher and his pinched lips parted.

'Why?' he croaked, into her face. 'Why do you hate me so much?'

The atmosphere amongst the group was taut and charged with expectancy. It seemed to me that the whole of Cloudrock was waiting for Catrunner's reply – birds, beasts and humans. Perhaps there were some among the Family that had guessed what I knew: that Catrunner had deliberately set out to murder her brother?

'We do not hate you – we love you,' she said at last, and smiled through the pain he was inflicting on her. She had cleverly included us all in her reply, though it was obvious to me that Stone's question had been directed at her only. I realized then that, in Catrunner, love and hate were fused emotions, almost to the point of being one. It was not that she couldn't tell the difference between them, or that they existed separately, but that they had absorbed each other and had evolved into a mutant emotion.

Stone's face changed to a look of terror and he gave out a long, low wail before sinking back, dead, onto the stretcher. Catrunner peeled his fingers from her wrist and I could see the blood where his nails had penetrated her flesh. She washed it in the stream while the rest of the Family waited for her to speak.

Finally she turned to the Greatgrandmother.

'We'll eat him tonight,' was all she said.

Woman: the womb and the tomb.

Chapter Seven

Back at the camp once again, the Family set about re-establishing the village and Clay was too busy to think too much about Tilana.

Not a single yurt had survived without some damage and most of the frames had disappeared completely. The skin coverings were still there, under the rock-weights, and they were the most important items. The canoes, like the skins, were undamaged, having been tethered to standing stones, but as Catrunner had predicted, the livestock had vanished.

The Family's first priority was to rebuild the yurts and those whose frames had survived almost intact helped those who had not a stick left standing. Since Clay's tent was one of those which required but a minimal amount of repair – a few lashings had come loose and one or two spars had snapped – my services were not required by him and I certainly was not going to help anyone else.

I went into the remains of the forest to look for domestic animals, knowing that some of them would have found shelter in holes or under shelves of rock. Those that I discovered I drove back to the village. The goats had been amongst the clever ones, and some of the fowls, but much of the livestock had been swept into the lake and had drowned. We could see their bodies drifting towards the rivers and streams, knowing they would be taken along these channels to be thrown out over the edge.

Not all the work was carried out peacefully and willingly, of course. The usual quarrels broke out between members of the Family who were working together: everyone wanted to do the job his or her way, and become thoroughly unreasonable when others thought differently.

Two weeks later, when the village was back to normal, hardly a member of the Family was on speaking terms with everyone else. The bickering had reached an unprecedented level at the end of each day, when, after hours of gruelling manual labour, there had been little to eat. Stone (the poison was of the kind that affected the blood, not the stomach) and the dead baby filled the women's larder for the first few days but the men had had to make do with roots and fish.

Clay remained aloof from the querulous atmosphere and seemed preoccupied most of the time. This was partly due to the fact that he was unwell and had to swallow a great deal of quassia. Quassia has a bitter, unpleasant taste but it does cure roundworm. Partly though, I knew he was thinking of Tilana and the hopelessness of such a friendship.

One evening, when the moon had arisen to illuminate the shattered forest, I went out hunting alone. I took my catapult and about a dozen round pebbles from the lakeshore. Making my way between the fallen trees, occasionally leaping from log to log, I paused every now and then to listen for the sound of prey. I sniffed the air for their scent.

The tree-frogs were making their usual din, accompanied by the cicadas and crickets, but my ears were sensitive, like a cat's, to that single discordant sound amongst all others in the world. It came, just as I was creeping along the bank of a rill and I stopped in my tracks, carefully placing a pebble in the saddle of my catapult. The sound came again, from just behind me, and I crouched low and sniffed the warm night air.

It was a human.

I quickly found a place in the cavity of two fallen trees that had crossed each other and were now locked.

The scent of woman. Strong. One of my own village. Fish and smoke, and that particular odour only a woman puts out. I waited, hoping she would pass by. Curious too. She was no hunter. Unskilled in stalking. There were too many rustles, cracks of twigs. The sound of a body brushing against branches.

'Dung-beetle!'

Du-u-unggg! Yellowbark, trying for a voice of honey, finding metal. Silence. The creatures around silenced by metallic tones. *Dung*! The sounding gong.

'Where are you, Dwarf?'

Dung-beetle. Dwarf. Someone speaking to me at last, but insults. Could not bring herself to treat me as equal. I peered out, saw her bulky form against the moon. Long hair lifting in the evening breeze. Piggy eyes glinted, searching, peering, surmising. The moon's light was on her skin.She looked more sallow than ever, suiting her name. Used to be *Cloudhair* but that turned to thatch. Hence the change.

At that moment I could have buried a stone in her temple. I drew back the catapult and took aim. Something held me back – a shadow of this shadow. The tension in my arm tired it quickly. To let go would be a relief, a release. I could excuse myself. Say it wasn't intended. Lie. I *wanted* to kill her. Gradually I relaxed and the tension went out of my arm. I was finished. I could never go back to the village. She would be there, ready to deliver the telling blow. *That's not a shadow, that's an unwanted. Over the cliff with it!*

'I want to know about Clay. I won't hurt you. I won't give you away. Tell me what he's up to? There's something wrong with him. You know what it's all about, Dwarf. Tell me . . .'

She moved nearer to a tall stump as she spoke. She thought she had my hiding place. Not quite, Yellowbark. Close. Rank sweat hit my nostrils. Armpit sweat. Crotch sweat. Foul. It overpowered the forest air, wrestled with the sweet scent of the grasses. She was impatient, her breath coming out in long, gaseous sighs.

Undertones. 'Come out you little . . .'

Then loudly, 'I'll give you presents. A bow. How would you like a bow?'

How would I like a bow? My straight eye for a bow: fair exchange. But my life? Not that. Not that, you old fishgutter. A hunter's weapon in her thick fisher's fist. And an arrow, ready. I studied her brute form, stark against the moon. Then drew back my catapult again.

Zing!

Off a trunk, close to her head. A long stream of curses came out, thrown up from the belly like vomit. Feel better Yellowbark, now its all up? All that bile? I too had to speak. Had to speak to a human for the first time in my life. My voice sounded strange.

'You fat sow. Now I have to go away – be separated from my brother. I hate you. Go away before I kill you. Send them after me – I don't care. I'll take you first . . .'

'Take me will you? What, here on the ground? And are you a man or a woman? Which? You'd like to know, eh?'

She cackled at her own deliberate misinterpretation of my

meaning as she turned her head towards the spot where I lay hidden.

This time I took careful aim at the side of her head and let fly a second shot. She shrieked with pain as the pebble clipped her left ear. Then, fumbling ineptly, she managed to discharge an arrow in my direction. I heard it penetrate a broken stump nearby and I gave out a terrible yell and thrashed around for a few moments before crawling to some other part of the undergrowth. She was shooting short at shadows.

I heard Yellowbark making her way to the crossed trees, muttering obscenities to herself. She searched around for a few minutes and then I heard her leave. No more arrows, apparently.

'Ram your bow up your unders!' I shouted triumphantly, 'You fungus-coloured fart!' This time I delighted in the sound of my own voice, but quickly became ashamed. Such stupidity was worthy only of the Family and I was sinking to their level in using such language.

For a long while I wandered around in thought. It seemed that I had broken free from the Family. I breathed in deeply, filling my lungs. The air of freedom was strong and I drugged myself with its strength. *Free.* My blood surged through my arteries, charged with bark-scented oxygen. Free. Free to do what? I did not know, but it made me lightheaded. My spirits were high, for a short while

I had prepared a hideout for such an event, in an old silk-cotton tree on the far side of the lake. How safe it would be I had no idea. Would they even bother to hunt me down? After all, I was less than nothing to them. What if Clay found me? Would he be piqued that I had deserted him and betray me to the Family? I knew he loved me but the Family circle was inviolate. Would he even miss his shadow?

The land crabs watched my progress round the lake with curiosity, their stalk eyes wavering at my approach and their brittle legs poised for flight should I venture too close. Cones of sand marked the entrance to their holes and I wished I had a little hole to crawl into. It would have been comforting to tuck myself into a ball in the close darkness of such a place.

How did the crabs see *me*? What filled their eyes?

45

A few nights previously I had heard Tilana ask Clay what he saw when he looked at me. He had replied with questions.

'What do you see when you catch a glimpse of a tree-spirit out of the corner of your eye? Can you describe the shape of the mist, or the form of a cloud? What do you hear when the breeze riffles the grass? How do you feel when the fire reaches out with unseen arms and folds you round with its warmth? Can you tell me how the moss smells when it dries under the sun? Or what colour the reflections of the stars are in the lake? Do not speak to me of my shadow. It is there, yet it is not there. Do you understand? . . .'

I walked first to the edge of Cloudrock. I had no particular reason for wanting to do this – except that I had some vague idea of trying to find a way to descend to the Deadlands below. It would offer, I hoped, an escape route at the very last resort.

I found a stream and followed its straight course with the moon at my back. My shadow walked out in front of me, tall and lean, like a hunter, like a slim, dark hunter. At that moment I was lord of the night, the lone adventurer full of confidence and strength.

Occasionally I heard the faint *plash* of a fish breaking water, interrupting the rhythm of the calling frogs. As I moved along the noise of these creatures paused until I was past, so that I was a moving island of silence in a lake of sound. Sometimes I caught the green gleam of a small tree-frog in the moonlight, or disturbed a grasshopper so that it whirred through the air in a long arc. We shared this world, they and I, that rose like an arm from the Deadworld, with the hand cupped, so that we could live out our lives on its palm, away from the horrors that dwelt below.

I reached the edge, where water from the stream shot out into space and then fell in mist-wrapped torrents to the place below. I studied the dark regions that spread in all directions beyond Cloudrock. Whenever I tried to think too hard about what lay beyond the beyond, my head would ring like struck metal and my brain would go dumb on itself.

Many rods separated me from the phantoms and the billowing water-smoke. Occasionally, the breezes blew an opening in the clouds of spray and I could make out tangled vegetation – dark, weird shapes of trees caught in struggles with wrestling vines. The floating mists covered and uncovered them at whim and their forms were indistinct, vague, blurred by the turbulence of the vapour. There was an opalescent sheen to the underclouds on moonlit nights which was both beautiful and mysterious and I wanted to reach down with long arms and gather the shining floss in my fingers. In the daytime, the floss changed to wild bands of colour: the decoys of the ghouls below, who tried to entice unwary souls to their lairs.

Deadworld!

'Deadworld. Where are my brothers and sisters? Where are you hiding my cousins?'

No answer.

The ghosts had no answer. They were good at listening, but tightlipped. Close. Full of secrets. Nothing *but* secrets. Secrets untold are useless things.

Something moved near my foot. A lump. A lump of clay rose into the air and *theump*, hit the ground.

'You can't frighten me,' I yelled, frightened.

Theump. Again. A clot of something. It landed on my foot. Squashy, pulpy mass. Cold. Slimy? No, dry. A toad, that was all. Nothing but a toad, pretending to be sinister. I picked it up and put it aside. It looked offended. Grey-green, it hunched into itself nursing its wrong and glaring at me with little, shiny eyes.

'Not my fault you're no ghoul,' I said. 'You ought to be grateful anyway. You're up here and they're down there.'

Things pretending to be other things. Was that me? An *unwanted*, pretending to be a real person? What was a real person? Clay. Tilana. Tall, sleek, perfect in limb. Me? Short, sturdy, one eye out of true. Inside? Were we different on the inside? Liver, heart, kidneys, bowels? No, the *other* inside. The deeper part. The thinking, feeling part. I did not believe so.

I could hear the wind, twisting and turning beneath the lip. I wished I could have seen what the wind had seen, then I would know. I would know if there was anything else out there, where my mind refused to go.

The Deadlands proper lay open to view: long, bleak flatlands where not a bush or tree could find a home. The flatlands went out to the horizon, with only the odd green blemish to break its ugliness. At night its dark hollows were haunted by horrible manifestations of the spirit world: cavorting, somersaulting and screaming their silent screams. Dogs could hear them. Cats could see them. Humans were deaf and blind to their antics, except when asleep. *Then* we saw them. Then we heard them. And these visions made us sweat terror from every pore.

There was a story told around the campfire that said that water once surrounded Cloudrock, came right up to its lip and went out on all sides into infinity. In those days the people of the island used to sail on boats across those waters to trade with other families in other places. But the sailors brought back with them many bad ways and Redgod, who can only be seen now as a vast smudge of ancestor blood-spirits, a dark or bright red, came down from the sky and dried up the water. To escape her anger the people of Cloudrock retreated into the caves and stayed there a long time before re-emerging. In order to keep her Families tied to the place of their birth she filled the Deadlands with terrible monsters and horrible traps which no human could survive for long.

We believed this story.

I slept that night in my moss-lined nest in the silk-cotton tree. The next morning I felt it was safe to venture out, for I knew it was a Bad Day and the Family would stay in their yurts. In our four-hundred-day year there were good and bad days occurring at regular intervals. Every ninth day was bad and no one would come looking for me on such a day. The majority of days were neutral, on which the forces of dark and light were equal. One could expect chance to play a bigger part on such days.

Bad Day or not I had to eat and I took my catapult to the edge of the lake where I knew some of the larger fish came to bask in the warm shallows. I sat in the fork of an overhanging tree and waited until a fish came drifting beneath me. I shook the tree gently so that several grubs fell from the leaves and plopped to the surface of the water. Soon, the fish rose and began eating them. As it turned for the third time, to snap a grub, I stunned it with a pebble and dropped into the water immediately to throw it onto the bank. There I ate most of it raw, saving a little for the evening meal.

The rest of the day I spent in gathering berries and roots, and generally making my nest as comfortable as possible. It felt very strange, living out there alone. Even though I was never part of the Family I had always been within the vicinity of the village and close to Clay. It was as if I had severed a cord and cut myself adrift. I felt I had no control over my movements. A kind of force, or current, was carrying me on its back.

There was no such thing as banishment from the Family. It was such an ugly, grotesque idea that its contemplation was unthinkable. Death was feared but its inevitability was accepted. Banishment was not a natural process and therefore not inevitable. It was abhorrent to the just and unjust alike. We had no word for it and members would indeed rather die than be cast out, if such a punishment were ever considered. (Even now that I have travelled and am aware of such a thing it still seems the cruellest of punitive actions.)

Perhaps Clay, if he ever thought of me at all, believed that I had crawled away to die somewhere, which is what he would have done if he had been sent away completely alone. That was something I was determined not to do. I would never pine away to death. I would live, despite the fact that I was alone.

What I did do was set about making myself a stool. I had never been allowed to own a stool before, which was reasonable since I could not expect to go to Redgod: the women would not eat me and in any case I was one of Her *unwanted*. The most I could hope for would be to return as a slug or snail but more than likely I would be a wandering spirit out on the Deadplace. Such creatures, slugs or ghosts, have no need for stools.

Yet I wanted one for my earthly life as a human. I could pretend I was a real person, destined for the sky.

I first fashioned some tools out of sharp stones, before setting to work. I knew it would be very rough-hewn and not at all like Clay's stool, but it would be *mine*. Perhaps when I was a slug, sliding around on the floor, I could think about my stool and know that I had left *something* behind, beneath Redgod's gaze? Something of the Shadow, in this world, where I never belonged except as a dark shape?

Chapter Eight

The loneliness became a physical pain.

The longer I spent alone, lying in the crutch of the great silk-cotton tree, the less inclined I became to hunt for my food. I had my stool, hidden in a crevice, but even the thought of that failed to lift my spirit. A depression settled on me which I could not shake off. I still kept company with the rocks, water and wind, but their presence was unsatisfying. I needed people around me, with voices and movement.

As the days passed I found myself wandering down to the shores of the lake to watch the distant canoes gliding like blunt-nosed beasts through the water. I kept hoping I would see Clay and perhaps permit him a sight of me so that I should not feel so utterly abandoned. I knew that Clay would not betray me. He was my brother.

Eventually I left the nest on a Bad Day and made my way back to the village. What I was going to do when I got there was not then a consideration. I just wanted to be close to people once again.

Already the foliage torn down by the great wind was beginning to grow tall again. The trees would take a long time, of course, but creepers and brambles had begun to re-establish their supremacy over the weaker flora. My lean brown arms had to busy themselves with clearing a path with a stone axe and it took me the best part of the day to reach the outskirts of the village.

The yurts had all been repaired and formed their three-ring target. Activity was in evidence in the doorways of yurts: people fashioning tools and sitting on their stools deep in conversation. The end of the day. Redgod was in full colour in the heavens and a dark, magenta glow was over the scene.

I sat and watched. Late in the evening I saw Clay creep from his yurt and into the damaged forest. I waited until he had passed me and then began to follow him. His long stride gave me trouble and I had difficulty in keeping up with him. Consequently I made more noise than I intended and I saw him stop and turn his handsome face my way. There was a look of fear in his features. He stared at the place where I had hidden and eventually I decided to risk showing myself. I rose slowly from a crouched position and watched the expression on my brother's face change from concern to puzzlement. We regarded each other for a few moments, then he turned and continued his walk.

I followed again, this time not bothering to conceal myself. Finally we came to a glade where, as I had expected, Tilana was waiting for him. He went directly to her and took her in his arms while I danced around in agitation on the edge of the clearing. Suddenly, Tilana pulled away from him.

'Who's that?' she said, with a tremor in her voice.

Clay waved his hand vaguely. 'It's only my shadow. No need to worry.'

'But . . . what if it tells someone? This is dangerous Clay. We must . . .'

Clay was tight-lipped as he replied. 'I see nothing but a shadow. Only fools are afraid of shadows.'

'Don't call me a fool.' Her voice was suddenly hard. 'This is stupid. It isn't sense to allow a third person into our secret. We should get rid of it now.'

'What? *What*?' He laughed.

She whirled away from him impatiently.

'This is all a mistake. I should never have come. What *am* I doing here? My brother . . .'

'Your brother. Your brother. I'm sick of hearing about your brother,' shouted Clay. 'I am a brother too – to that – that – that standing over there. What? Do you think I can kill? Here . . .' He thrust a knife into her hand. 'You – you go and kill my shadow. Yes, it's easy isn't it? You just run over and stick the blade in its belly and watch the blood spurt out. It must be easy. You think I can do it just like that. Kill it then!'

Tilana stood for a moment holding the blade loosely in her hand. I was all nerves and taut tendons, poised ready for flight. Clay knew she would never catch me. He would not have given her the knife if he was not sure of that.

Finally she let the knife fall to the ground.

'Shadows don't bleed,' she said, softly.

Clay said, 'I bleed.'

She turned her attention to him again, apparently forgetting about me.

'I know, but I must marry my brother. You must marry your mother. This is the way it has to be. I must bleed too, on my wedding night. You know that. Afterwards it will not matter and we can do what we want, but not before. Not before.'

Clay was white and shaking, his fists clenched. He said in distressed tones, 'Don't talk about that. Don't speak of him – and you, doing that. I can't – even the thought of him *touching* you makes me feel sick.'

It was a dance. A dance of words and feelings. Back two steps, forward one, turn around, walk away, whirl, back to the first position. The insects do it, testing each other. The birds do it, to attract. All of them have their tricks of movement and their voices of mating. Some of them clown. Some of them weave serious suggestions in the air. Conscious, unconscious.

Also the natural tricks.

Eyes.

Concentrate on the eyes. Bright eyes. Sultry eyes. A flicker here, for coyness. A pretence at shyness. Eyes wide and round. Eyes narrowed and promising.

Smell.

The odour of sex. The false scents, gathered from other sources. Let it waft to the partner. *How I love the smell of your skin.* Dangerous smells, to intimidate. Enticing smells. *Come to me. Come to me.*

Touch.

A light brush against the arm. Warm. *Feel that warmth? You could have it all – the heat of the body.* A hand, clutching the wrist. Strong. Protective. The returning touch. Sympathetic. *Let me look after you.* The forbidden touch. *Not there, not there.* Where? *Oh, yes! There. There.*

Taste.

Salty, on the skin. Lips shivering against the shoulder. Perspiration of the other on the tongue.

I watched it all happening and overpowering it, the sense of not being able to possess, absolutely. The whole world, forcing its way between them, massive and immovable. A taboo, solid as rock. My brother was helpless. He bent over, clutching his breast and moaning. 'Oh no. I don't want to – I don't want you to – why does it have to be this way? My *mother*. I loathe my mother. I want you. I do. I do.' He suddenly became fierce. 'I will *kill* your brother. I will kill them both.'

She took his head in her arms as he sank to the floor in front of her, pressing it against her abdomen. I expected her to be shocked, angry, but she seemed solicitous. Her long black hair fell about his shoulders, as she rocked him, whispering, 'Clay, Clay. Don't worry. We'll always know each other. We must do what they tell us and keep our secret. Perhaps, one day, we'll find a way to be together all the time. I don't know how, but we'll find a way.'

They stood, like two tall trees, in the moonlight. Two silver trees that have grown side by side, their roots locked together, for the whole of their lives. To uproot one would be to destroy them both. I felt their sorrow in my blood and it was *deep*. How they could love each other was beyond my understanding. It was inconceivable that they should feel that way about someone not of their own blood, but they did. They *did* feel this impossible thing. I could feel the atmosphere charged with emotion, like the air before a storm which makes my hair crackle. It was as if they were the centre of such a storm and the energy of their love destroyed everything around them.

'What are we going to do?' asked Clay, miserably. 'I would die for you – you know that. Please, Tilana.'

She touched his cheek, stroked it.

'We must be sensible. This is wrong. You know it and I know it. But we can't help ourselves. It is the strongest taboo we have and Redgod must be very angry with us. Yet, if we did not meet again I know I would despair. We must meet – because we *have* to.'

Clay began crying and I clutched my stomach, feeling the agony of his unhappiness. Poor Clay. My brother. My brother.

'Can't we go away somewhere?' He said through the tears. 'There must be somewhere. Some secret place where no one would find us?'

She shook her head.

'Nowhere. They would find us in the end and I – I don't want to die. I'm sorry. I'm not as strong as you. I'm afraid, for both of us. I don't want anything to happen to you either.'

They lay down on the grass then and I felt the hopelessness of it all wash over me. Their passion was new. They could not have each other and the unobtainable always heightens passion. Of course it was wrong, but sometimes the individual *wrong* is greater in power than the collective *right*.

The night passed with the lovers wrapped in each other's arms, while I sat guarding them. Around them creatures made love in wild abandon, free to do as they wished with their bodies. It all seemed so unbalanced. Were I a magician I would have had no hesitation in changing them into a pair of grasshoppers for the night and then *they* could have done as they wished.

Dawn came as an angry flood of scarlet: it moved across the sky with heads of dogs and the wings of birds. The soft, warm shadows of the moonlit forest melted away and sharper, harder shadows took their places. The damp smells of the night dissipated in the morning air – made way for the thick odours of the day. I could smell the grasses drying and could hear the soft crackle of the leaves unfolding. Birds began strutting along branches, greeting each other: myriads of insects awoke from a short sleep. Not far from me the two miscreants slept. The morning horn sounded.

Tilana leapt to her feet instantly.

'I must go.'

Clay dragged himself dispiritedly to an upright position. 'I suppose so. When?'

'Not tonight. I should be missed. There is a marriage feast . . .'

He nodded.

She took his face in her hands and a look of pain came into her eyes.

'Two days time. I shall be hunting on the far side of the island. By the black Wedding Rock. Perhaps you'll be there too . . . ?'

'I shall be there,' he replied.

Then she was gone, into the broken trees, like a two-legged cat. Clay stood for a long while staring at the place where she had entered the forest, then, as if someone had struck him in the back, he straightened his posture and some urgency entered his demeanour. Now that Tilana had gone he was worrying about whether he had been missed or not. He still had that air of misery about him. There was a brokenness to his walk, as if he were labouring under a heavy load. I longed to give him comfort and ran to him, leaping onto his back. I wrapped my arms around his head, as I used to of old. He barely paused in his pace. Breaking our normal rule of silence I began humming a tune I had learned from a little rill on the far side of the lake. It was a solemn melody but I wanted him to know that I sympathized with his distress, even if the source of the melancholy was unlawful.

Before we reached the village I dropped from his shoulders and crept away into the forest, making tracks for my nest in the silk-cotton tree. On reaching my home I immediately began digging beneath an outcrop of rock. The earth that came from this exercise I carried to the lake and scattered on its waters. Then I began gathering stout branches to use as shoring timbers. I knew what I wanted to do to help my brother.

Over the next two days I reinforced the roof and walls of the large hole I had dug. I then lined it with soft grass. It was to be a hideout when the lovers needed it, as I knew they must one day. Such liaisons cannot go unnoticed forever. Tilana knew that. When I had finished camouflaging the entrance, I brushed away my tracks from the surrounds of the rock. The place would be there when it was required.

'Well,' I said to the wind, 'I've done my best. Now we shall have to wait and see what happens. I no longer feel lonely – perhaps because I know that loneliness is not the worst thing in the world. Something else is.'

The wind was non-committal. Ambiguity suits its character. How I envied the creatures of the wind: the hawk, the bat, the seagull. How they mastered the master.

'One day,' I promised.

And the wind agreed. Or perhaps not? One can never tell with the wind.

Chapter Nine

The day arrived when I saw the preparations for Clay's wedding taking place. A huge fire was being built in the centre of the village and two ornately carved wedding canoes bobbed gently on the lake. From a hiding-place just outside the tents I observed Clay sitting on his stool outside his yurt.

There was a mountain on his shoulders. He looked bowed and dejected and even the parrot's feathers which decorated his hair, neck and waist seemed to droop in sympathy with his low spirit. Yellowbark sat close by him, occasionally glancing at his face with a quizzical look. What reason he had given for his depression I had no idea, but it was impossible to hide emotions within the Family group.

It was normal for a young man about to be married to be excited, if not ecstatically happy. If nothing else the anticipation of his first sexual experience should have put him on edge. Instead, here was a youth with a face like a wet drumskin. Surely Catrunner must have been angry with him? And Yellowbark, judging by her glances, was highly suspicious as to the cause of his unhappiness. I heard her say something about 'pining' once, but Clay merely shook his head in response. I wondered if that had anything to do with me.

At midday, Clay rose and went to the ancestor's log at the back of the village, where he approached the black stools with a bowed head, shuffling forward on his knees. I knew what he would be praying for and I knew that it would not be granted: Redgod was not going to answer a prayer which flouted her own laws.

An idea occurred to me at that moment. I had been trying to work out a way to get a message to him regarding the hideout I had arranged for him and Tilana. It was unthinkable that I should speak to him directly – but one of his ancestors could do it.

I crept around the village and behind the giant log. I could not see Clay but I knew he was there, and called out softly, 'Clay, this is your father. If you are in need of a place to hide, go to your shadow who lives in the silk-cotton tree on the far side of the lake.' I repeated the instruction twice. Then I crept back to my original position, to see what effect my words had had on him.

He was kneeling before his father's stool with a stupefied expression on his face. Once or twice he glanced over his shoulder, either to see if anyone else had heard, or to ascertain whether any chicanery was involved. It was difficult to tell. At least the trick had chased away his depression for a while.

Catrunner then came. She too approached the log on her knees and moved up alongside Clay. I saw her whisper into his ear and he leaned on her shoulder a little. For the moment, they were mother and son, the latter seeking comfort in his parent's presence.

That which was to come – husband-son, mother-wife – was not just a matter of establishing another tie between them, but of tangling many lines. His father, though dead, would not be viewed in the same light as he had been before. His responses to his mother's affections would be caught between those of a lover and those of a dutiful son. The woman that had told him stories as a child; that had sung him to sleep; that had protected him; that had advised him, petted him, scolded him – that same woman would be looking for strength from him. She would be looking for a lover's abilities to satisfy both her spiritual and physical needs. She would be seeking love of a very different kind. And he? He would have no mother to turn to if a crisis point was reached in his marriage, just as she would have no son to support her when her husband failed to reach some crucial understanding that was necessary to her. They were one and the same. Both.

I left them there in the last glow of parent-child relationship and made my way to the lakeside. I wanted to find a vantage point where I could observe the canoes when they went out onto the water for the vigil. The day was Good, of course, chosen for the purpose. The silk-cotton tree was as high as any.

On arriving back, I found my nest occupied. A wildcat sat in the fork, cleaning its paws. It regarded me steadily as I approached. Was I merely a passer-by or was I a threat? When it saw that I was not moving on, its point of interest changed to same vague, distant horizon. I have noticed this about cats: if you don't go away of your own accord they remove you from the world. You cease to exist. I was used to such treatment. I knew that anything I did – I could stand on my head and wave my arms – its attention would still remain on that indefinite object somewhere beyond my left shoulder.

Since I had not got my catapult with me I began to climb the tree – cautiously. It moved then, casually walking out onto a branch as if that had been its intention the whole time and its decision to do it at that moment, just as I was climbing the tree, was pure coincidence. It settled down, further along the bough, with its back to me, totally disregarding my presence. I could see its left ear twitching as it watched a humming bird dangling from an invisible thread above a scarlet blossom. Yet I knew its every muscle was tensed and ready for flight, even though it appeared relaxed.

'You can't fool me,' I said.

There was a flick from its tail and then we forgot about each other.

By mid-afternoon the canoes were out on the lake. The vigil had begun. Purification. How? How was he going to do it? By lingering until he was too tired to tell the difference between good and bad thoughts? Catrunner would be impatient. They would clash.

All day. All day, drifting aimlessly. Sunlight glancing from the water. Blinding. Then twilight. Then the stars, taking their places. First one. Then twothreefourfive. Then the final rush until the sky sparkled. Moonrise, moonfall. Rats plopping into the lake. Frog chorus. Otherwise, stillness. Trees printing different patterns on the water. The wildcat, slinking off to hunt.

I made a raft. It would just take my prone weight. I began paddling towards the centre of the lake, careful not to make splashing sounds. There had been many logs and broken trees in the lake since the wind. I disguised myself with driftwood. I felt that, even in the moonlight, I could pass as a piece of flotsam.

As I approached the canoes I was struck by the complete silence. The vigil was, of course, supposed to be conducted in quiet, but when two people were about to be married they inevitably conversed for some of the time, seeking assurances from one another. I floated close by them.

Catrunner was draped over the bow of her vessel, one hand dangling in the water. Clay was sitting bolt upright in his canoe, looking at the shore, sullenly.

A groan escaped the lips of Catrunner.

Then words, almost inaudible to me.

'I'm your *mother*.'

There was no answer from Clay. He looked as if he had just been moulded from the substance that made his name. The canoes were very close together, side touching side. The wood seemed more sentient than the occupants. The two canoes bumped lightly, as if seeking reassurance from each other.

Catrunner again. 'Why? What are you doing to me? I don't understand what's happened to you, Clay. Can't you talk to me? Please talk to me? – Look, son! *Look at me!*' Her voice rose dramatically. 'By my life, if you don't look at me I'll crack you such a ... Are you listening to me? How *dare* you ignore me. How *dare* you. I won't have it, child. Respect. I will have respect from you, if nothing else. I'm *talking* to you.'

'I hear you mother.'

The wheedling tone again. 'Oh, Clay, don't let's fight. This is our wedding. Just tell me what's wrong. Why can't we go in and get on with the rest of the ceremony? They'll all be waiting. We've kept them waiting too long now, don't you see? Let's go back now. Here, give me your hand ...'

'No!'

She suddenly sat up, her face becoming very fierce in the moonlight. I thought she had seen me. But she screamed at Clay instead.

'You'll do as you're told, boy. We'll go back *now* ...' She choked the words out. '... and ... you'll finish the ceremony. Let's have no more stupidity.'

'I *cannot* go back impure.' Clay was emphatic and I knew his confidence surprised her because she let out a little sound, halfway between a sob and a cry of pain.

'How impure? How?'

No answer. Above us and around us, the sky. There were no horizons. Even below us was sky – the bottom of the sky, but, nevertheless. Just we three then, floating above the world, like travellers on cloud. Two of us waiting for an answer, and none coming.

Finally. 'I'm impure because I have had bad thoughts. Unworthy. I'm not worthy, mother. I don't want to get married – ever. These bad thoughts . . . '

'What is it?' insisted Catrunner.

'I . . . I think about someone else.'

There was silence – a terrible silence in which Catrunner was trying to absorb these cruel words.

'Who?' she said, bleakly.

No answer.

'Who, Clay? Who is it? One of your young cousins? I know I'm old to you, but really . . . ' Her voice began to falter. Even in the moonlight I could see her complexion was as white as wood-ashes. 'Tell me.'

There was sadness in her voice and Clay must have sensed a sympathy for his dilemma. He had tortured himself too long and the need to unburden his guilt was apparently overpowering. I could see by his expression that he was going to breach the dam, let it all come flooding out. I wanted to warn him, but of course I couldn't. He gave way to imprudence, believing, I suppose, and wrongly, that maternal instincts would prevail over what was right. That a mother's understanding and forgiveness would be stronger than her jealousy.

He said. 'It's no one in the Family.'

I felt as though I had a rock caught in my throat. She would surely kill him? I knew she had the ritual knife for the bloodmingling and I waited for the soft, sucking sound that meant it had been plunged into his belly. Instead she let out a hysterical laugh.

'Don't be ridiculous.'

Wisely, Clay remained silent.

Catrunner began a one-sided conversation.

'Why, there's no such thing. You can't want someone outside the Family – that wouldn't be love, it would be – something disgusting. What you mean is you've made a friend of – of someone in the Night Family. Someone – yes. You met someone that night we slept in their caves – and you made a friend. You can have a friend son, however unusual it is. Can't you see how fond I am of you?'

'Can I really?' he said, too eagerly. 'Can I really see her . . .?'
The words gushed out. 'She's beautiful mother. *You* must see her
. . .'

'Beautiful?' The word was taut and again I wanted to warn
him, warn my brother not to go any further.

'Oh, yes. She's the most beautiful girl on Cloudrock. Her eyes
. . .'

Catrunner's voice became thin and shrill.

'Have you . . . Have you done anything?'

If Clay had not been so surprised by the sudden change in
tone, he might have answered truthfully, *no*. Instead he became
confused and began blurting out phrases like, 'We see each other
– we talk. She tells me things. I like her – she's so soft and warm.
We go places together, and hunt. Her skin is like – is like . . .'

'You *animal!*'

Catrunner reached over, almost capsizing her canoe, and
gripped his hair. Then she cracked him viciously across the face
with her hand. The sound echoed over the water. There was a
brief struggle as he tried to ward off further attacks of nails and
blows, and all the while Catrunner was screaming at him,
unintelligible curses. I wondered about the rest of the Family.
They were surely gathered on the bank listening to this ugly
exchange. Perhaps their canoes would soon be cutting through
the water towards us? I was frightened, both for Clay and
myself. The vigil was sacred and was supposed to remain
undisturbed but such a scene was unusual, to say the least.

Catrunner began sobbing and suddenly produced the knife. I
held my breath.

She muttered to herself. 'We *will* do this thing. Love? You
stupid boy. The sort of thing you're talking about is like – like a
hawk mating with a wildcat. It's ugly – and the offspring would
be ugly. This has got to be stopped. We will mingle our blood –
now!

I saw her draw the blade across her wrist, but she was shaking
violently. She let out a long sigh then, and I guessed that she had
made the cut too deep. The blood spurted out in a long, thin
stream and hit the water close to me.

Clay had begun paddling away from her and the sound of the
blood splashing on the surface was lost in the noise of the blade
striking the water.

'Clay?' she cried in an alarmed voice.

He continued, further out onto the lake.

'I'm hurt.'

He ignored her, perhaps misinterpreting the words. I could hear him sobbing to himself, lost in his own self-pity. Then he let himself drift, his face buried in his hands. They were several rods apart and I saw Catrunner attempt to move towards him but the paddle slipped out of her bloodwet hands. She moaned loudly and called his name twice more. Still he ignored her.

'You've hurt me,' she cried, and tried paddling the canoe nearer to him with her hands. 'Please help me.'

The wedding canoe was unwieldy – a heavy craft not fashioned for speed, or manoeuvrability. Her awkward attempts at closing the distance between them was frustrated by the snaking movements of the unmanageable boat. I saw her growing weaker and the urge to help overwhelmed my natural state of remaining inconspicuous. She was my mother.

I steered my raft towards her canoe, moving as fast as I could. Speed was not easy, lying on my belly and awash with water. By the time I reached her all I could hear was shallow breathing. I gripped the edge of the canoe and looked inside.

She was lying full length on the bottom, her eyes open, staring at the sky. Her breast was rising and falling laboriously. She looked peaceful enough – almost as if she had chosen to lie down and rest in a pool of her own blood.

I wanted to speak, but the words would not come. What could I do to help? She had to tell me what to do. But all she did was to stare up at the sky. Inside, I felt two separate instincts pulling strongly in opposite directions. One part of me cried, 'She's your mother. Find the words! Do it!' While the other part asserted itself by withholding my power of speech.

Her breathing seemed to stop, yet she was still alive because her eyelids flickered occasionally. I became angry with myself for my inadequacy and frantic at the thought that I was allowing someone to die. Yet still the words would not form. In my frustration, I hammered on the side of the boat.

She looked at me then, with a glimmer of recognition. Her eyes suddenly went very bleak. She moved, as if she were struggling with some inner feeling that was so strong it needed physical repression. I waited for her to say something, or give me some sign. All I needed was an indication of what I was to do. She would not last until I got her to the shore. Her breath came back. She gulped down air and released it in noisy grunts. A spasm went through her body again, as if some deeply rooted inner force were at work. One of her hands fluttered like a wounded bird. With great effort apparent in her features she raised her arm and gripped the edge of the canoe. Gradually her fingers worked their way along the lip until they touched mine. They rested there for an instant. A strange light came into her eyes, frightening in its fever.

Her fingers sought my own. With a strength I found alarming she gradually peeled my hand from the edge of the boat. I drifted away from her with those fierce eyes still blazing into my own. Then they were gone from my sight.

A moment later the breathing stopped.

I felt devastated. Even in death. Even, in death. She would accept nothing from an unwanted child.

The moonlight was pale on the water. Clay sat hunched in his own craft, as still as if he had been carved from wood: a dark, chiselled shape against the night. A breeze sprang up and ripples began racing each other across the surface.

I looked up at the moon. There was a frown upon its visage and a terrible look of enquiry in its eye. In the distant trees was a whisper, far off. Terrible creeds were being recited amongst the woodland grasses. Incantations were murmured into the night air.

'I'm sorry, mother,' said Clay.

Chapter Ten

Suddenly, it was blackless.

It was a strange sky, mottled and brooding: a twilight that was not evening. Clay was deathless, so was I. The other canoe drifted slowly in circles, carrying its unliving load. Around us the water was not without colour and fish that swam into its clouds suddenly went blind. The moon had gone. The stars, in secret holes. If we were slow we would be caught.

I paddled to Catrunner's craft. Clay was already there, looking down on her. He reached out and touched her forearm, then retracted his hand instantly. He glanced towards the shore, then back at the pastel face with its slack mouth. He lifted one of her hands and let it fall. Then he gave a cry, grabbed a handful of her hair and banged her head twice against the wood, before putting the mouth close to his ear and listening.

I climbed into his canoe, picked up the paddle and propelled us towards the shore farthest from the village. Clay crouched for a leap, between the two canoes but the distance was too great. He slumped down in the bottom of the boat and seemed vaguely interested in the grain of the wood. I hoped he would stay quiet. Although Catrunner's death had been an accident, Clay, like anyone else, had his enemies in the Family. I had to get him to safety until tempers cooled.

As I paddled I experienced new feelings: sorrow and guilt over the death of another. How could I have saved her? I could not have got her to shore in time and I was unskilled at doctoring severed arteries. I could, I suppose, have applied some sort of initial aid, but she had refused it. Now she was gone, the woman that had abandoned me as a baby and had ignored my upbringing. She had severed relationships with the umbilical cord and in truth her death was no more a parting than if we had lived a thousand miles away from one another.

We reached the bank. I led Clay to the hideout, but he wasn't eager to enter. I left him for a while, returning to the canoe to send it on a course for the Deadplace along a stream. When I got back he was in the hole. I passed him some fruit and a gourd of water, then covered the entrance with fresh branches.

I wondered what was going through my brother's mind. He knew they would hunt him down. I was in greater danger now than I had ever been. They couldn't care less about me, but a real person like Clay was a different matter. They would want to know why Clay did not summon assistance for his mother. One way and another they would discover his crime: that of falling in love with someone outside the Family. I could see nothing but tragedy ahead.

I sat in my nest and studied the kites as they circled Catrunner's canoe. Soon afterwards the lake was filled with boats and I knew the search would begin. I prepared myself for a long wait.

I awoke at midday to the sound of running feet and peered through the leaves. There were two hunters prowling around the base of the tree – a man and a woman. Bluewater and Quickhand, her husband-brother. They both stared up into the branches of the silk-cotton and I remained very still. Soon afterwards Bluewater left and Quickhand seemed to settle down to rest in the shade. I could see the tip of his spear, but the man himself was directly underneath and hidden from view. A little while later I heard the sound of eating and drinking.

I prayed that Clay, some two rods away, would keep silent. There was nothing to do but wait out the day. It was hot in my nest and during the course of the afternoon insects and spiders used my body as a waterhole, drinking my perspiration as it ran down my body. Quickhand seemed in no hurry to leave and by late afternoon I was beginning to fear he would stay all night. He was one of those slow, methodical men who undertake a task with the patience of the sun. Time meant nothing to him, so long as the job was done to his satisfaction. He was always last in everything, so that he exasperated all around him, until their nerves reached snapping point and they could not care less about perfection, so long as he finished quickly.

He never did. He laboured, long and long, until all interest of others had waned, and no one gave the artifact a second glance. Yet, paradoxically, he could be lightning fast when it came to a single, instinctive movement. He could snatch a fly in flight, or a snake in mid-strike. His name could be used in admiration, or with heavy irony.

Suddenly he stirred and appeared in view again. My heart began to bang against my ribs as he looked towards the hideout where Clay lay hidden.

Had he heard a sound? What was it? Just then the wildcat passed by, a rod from Clay's hole. Quickhand picked up a stone and threw it hard at the beast. It turned and hissed as the missile skimmed its flank. It looked for cover.

Don't use the hole, I thought.

But the cat bolted off towards a tangle of broken trees. Quickhand, however, continued to stand, still looking in Clay's direction. *What was it?*

He had seen something. I studied the place where the pit lay hidden and my heart skipped as I realized what had attracted his attention. The leaves of the branches I had covered Clay's hiding place with were beginning to crisp and wither. Their silver undersides were showing as they curled into rolls, making them stand out against the live shrubs around the hole like pampas plumes against a curtain of dark trees.

Quickhand began to walk slowly towards the dead branches, his spear held javelin-like in his right hand. I fitted a pebble to my catapult and eased myself out of my nest on to a branch. Then I took aim and fired.

I honestly intended to clip the side of his head and stun him, but for once my aim was untrue. The stone struck him at the base of his skull. He dropped with a little sigh. I scrambled down the trunk just as Clay emerged from his hole. He had a rock in his hand.

We both bent over the body. It did not take long to establish that Quickhand was dead. *I had killed someone.* I felt sick inside. I, who did not like killing anything, not even an animal unless it were for food, had killed one of my kin. No longer would he make jokes at the camp fire about how he caught snakes by their tails and kissed their heads without being bitten. No longer would he grumble about the thickness of the porridge, the fattiness of the steak, the thinness of the stew. No longer would his wife-sister, Bluewater, feel his warm, lean body close to hers in the yurt at night. He was dead. Killed by a shadow.

Practical issues entered my thoughts. We had to get rid of the

66

body. The Family would search the area where Bluewater had left him, leaving nothing overlooked. They would find him and see the cause of death. I was the only one on Cloudrock with a catapult.

We could have carried the corpse between us and thrown it over the edge, but that would have meant the women would be unable to eat the remains. Quickhand would be robbed of his afterlife. I couldn't do that to him. The snake killer was dead and I was responsible. He didn't deserve to be cast out of the Family forever.

The *snake killer* . . . I had an idea. I motioned to Clay to return to his hole. He seemed reluctant at first, but eventually retired from my sight. I covered his hideout with fresh leaves, throwing the others well away.

I then inspected Quickhand's wound. There was only one small clot of blood: the stone was buried deep in his neck. I rubbed dirt over the wound. Then I dragged him to the base of the silk-cotton and propped him up in a sitting position against the trunk. I broke off two long barbs from a poison thorn bush and pierced his flesh with them, side by side, on a prominent part of his leg. Luckily the blood was still warm and two fang-like incisions showed plainly against the brown skin. *Not good enough*, I thought as I inspected him.

I took a rock and beat the flesh on and around the wound until it looked blue, if not swollen. Then I took my loin cloth, rolled it into a tube and made faint snake tracks in the dust near his leg. Finally I retrieved his spear and placed it across his knees.

Still he looked too posed. A man with a snake bite doesn't stay sitting where he is. After the initial panic he tries to do something about it. He had no knife, so he could not lance the wound. What, then, would he do? A tourniquet probably, to stop the poison reaching his heart. I took the cord out of his loin-cloth and with a twig made a tourniquet on his thigh. Then I placed his right hand on the twisted handle. It fell away, but that didn't matter. It looked more natural. There were virulent snakes that could kill in minutes. This had been done by one of those.

Though the task was gory I have to say the finished work was artistic. I added one small touch. I placed his left hand, palm down and gripping some dust, to emphasize the pain he had suffered. Then I climbed back up into my nest, leaving the poor exhibit on show. I was not particularly proud of my newly discovered talent, but I felt it was good enough to fool the Family.

My guile appeared to work. Bluewater returned and at first she thought Quickhand was asleep, for she smiled and touched his face to wake him. It was twilight and the colours of the sky reflected on Quickhand's skin, serving to disguise his wounds until she made a closer inspection in the dim light. On discovering the punctures decorated with blue-black bruises, she let out an awful wail that echoed over the lake. Guilt came flooding into my heart as I watched her beating the ground with her fists and releasing her grief into the still evening. At that moment I would have done almost anything to breathe new breath into Quickhand's body. Instead, he lay like a slim branch that has been struck with an axe, once or twice in its centre, and has been creased and doubled up.

Bluewater left, still moaning loudly.

Later, some hunters returned and bore the body away. I followed them, leaving Clay where he was, back to the village. There was a fire going in the centre of the yurts and the women were clustered around it with expectant looks on their faces. Quickhand was to be eaten immediately. I could see the firelight shining on the skins of those about to eat his flesh.

In one of the yurts the men would be ritually preparing the meat. They would, no doubt, be stripping out those parts infected with the poison. These would be burnt on the fire along with the bones. They would be carried up to Redgod as smoke. Bones do not easily burn and it would take several days to reduce them to ashes in the charcoal. Already Bluewater was staining his stool black, sobbing as she did so, ready to place it on the ancestor's log.

Not long afterwards the smell of roast pork was wafting through the remains of the forest on the back of the evening breeze and I heard the sounds of eating: lips smacking together, belches and the tearing of half-cooked flesh from bone. I crawled closer.

I heard Yellowbark say, 'She's as tough now as she was in life. Gaaaahhh! Full of string . . .'

I suddenly realized that they were eating Catrunner as well as Quickhand. They would be bloated by the morning.

Yellowbark was picking her teeth when I next dared to look. Someone said, 'She used to get in our hair, now she's getting in between our teeth.' An old woman laughed. These fireside jokes, while eating another Family member, were part of the ritual. It was traditional and in no way disrespectful of the dead.

Suddenly, there was a commotion from the butcher's yurt and a man ran across the village to the circle round the fire. He held Quickhand's head in his hand by the hair.

'Killed . . .' I heard him say. 'Pebble.'

'Where?' Yellowbark was on her feet and inspecting the severed head.

'Look, here,' cried the butcher. 'There's a hole. I got this out of it . . .' He extended his palm dramatically.

'The dwarf,' shouted Yellowbark. 'Nearly killed me once with that catapult. Clay must have gone to that ugly toad and together they murdered poor Quickhand. We have to find them . . .'

They would not look for us at night. Firstly, the feast could not be interrupted, and secondly they would need daylight.

As I ran away I heard Yellowbark screeching, 'That worm. We should have left it where it was found. Or tossed it over the edge. I told you it was evil, but no one takes notice of what I say. Spawned by a tree-toad that one. Gaahh!'

'It was Catrunner,' someone replied. 'She said it might be . . .' But I never heard the rest. What were they talking about? Not me surely. My mother was Catrunner and they all knew it.

I hurried back to Clay. We had to find a new hiding-place before dawn. He was fast asleep when I found him and did not seem inclined to move, but I destroyed his hiding-place around him. Reluctantly he climbed to his feet and we set out at a fast walk to the edge of the world.

We searched all night and finally found a ledge beside a waterfall. We climbed down beneath it, slowly. I remember thinking: one slip and I'll end up in the very place I avoided at birth.

There was a small cavity beneath the ledge, just big enough for us to lie down in, side by side. We did so, clutching each other for support and security. I soon fell asleep.

Chapter Eleven

The next day passed without us being discovered. Clay seemed disinclined to move anyway. He just lay on his side, his head cupped in his hand, and stared out over the Deadlands. Some hunters came close to us, but passed by without looking beneath the ledge.

That night I went out and gathered some roots and berries for us to eat. Clay contributed nothing, but I guessed he was not yet over his mother's death and would eventually show some of his old vitality, once the grief began to recede.

This did not happen.

Day after day he just lay there and apart from eating and drinking, did nothing. In losing his mother he seemed to have lost himself. I saw him sinking deeper and deeper into despair and realized that if I could not rouse him to some kind of action he would die. He would grey into death: not the first to fade away from doing nothing. His whole existence seemed to be centred on the Deadplace, which he stared at, morosely, over the whole time. It was as if he had decided that this was his spiritual home: that he was destined for the mists far below us.

I continued to forage for both of us, but our diet was not good and may have contributed to his despondency. Only occasionally was I able to bring back meat, unless it was a scrap of a frog, or crushed termites. I was not a good night hunter and my prey knew better than I the night trails. We could not exist as we were indefinitely and I began to get concerned.

Every night I tried to persuade Clay to come hunting by tugging at his arm, but he continued to stare down into the vapours below, resisting any attempt to move him. It would have been dangerous, taking him out in the condition he was in but I felt that anything would have been better than just watching him waste away.

Then, one night, he responded.

I pulled at his wrist, not expecting anything but a scowl and a grunt, when he looked up, climbed shakily to his feet and followed me to the top. It was as if something inside him had clicked back into place and he was once more the brother I knew. Hollow-eyed, and wan, but the old Clay. There was an intent look in his eyes that, had I been fully alert, I should have recognized.

We began walking and he set off at a fast pace. I saw him glance up at the sky once or twice and nod his head as if confirming something. He strode out in front of me as if he had a purpose. I had thought previously that when he did come out he would trail behind me in the same kind of trance shown since the death of Catrunner. Not so. Instead, it was me hurrying to keep up with *him*.

Where was he going? Why did he look so determined? I began to feel unease. There was something about his pace that spelled urgency, immediacy. What? I hadn't even realized he was counting the days. He had seemed so immersed in himself, I thought that time had been forgotten.

Gaunt and tight-lipped, he strode towards a place unfamiliar to me and the rest of the Family. I knew what was there though and my heart sank. Soon the tall pinnacle came into view: the Wedding Rock of the Night Family. Instead of floating on the lake they carried out their vigil here. Now I knew what day it was: Tilana's wedding day. Or rather, night. This was the time when she and her brother would be married.

No! Not more trouble. We were saturated in problems already and now my brother was out to create more.

I tried to hold him back by the wrist. He shook me off, violently, not even pausing in his stride. No one could have stopped him at that moment. Had a mountain dropped on the path in front he would have dug through it with his fingers. Nothing short of death was going to get in his way.

We came to the clearing where the rock stood like a tall broken tree open to the night. The moonlight shone on two figures on top. They were sitting side by side, quite still, looking into the face of the moon. The scene was idyllic and I was horrified to think that it might soon be transformed into a carnage. Overhead, dark clouds were gathering. There would be a heavy rain in the morning – if we ever saw another morning. A sound from

71

the corner of the rock told me that a southerly wind was gathering in strength.

Clay stared up at the figures above, then reached out for my catapult. I snatched it back from him. He was not going to murder someone else with my weapon. He gave me a pained look, then focused his attention on the rock again. Before I realized his intention he had crossed the clearing and was silently climbing the tall stone, like a dumb monkey shinning up a tree trunk.

He moved like a shadow, a dark figure against the darker rock. I was afraid for him in case he should fall and almost let out a cheer when he reached the summit. I saw him stand there, behind the sitting figures, tall and straight now, like a rock himself – hard, powerful, full of strength.

In that moment it seemed to me that all Cloudrock was waiting, holding its breath. No crickets chirruped; no tree-frogs sang; the wind had dropped. Clouds were frozen in their positions, as were streams and rills. The whole forest waited, expectantly. All knew that Clay was about the disrupt a wedding vigil.

The heart of the world had stopped in mid-beat.

When Clay stepped forward, there was a struggle during which two figures blended. I had no idea which was which. There was grunting above me, as muscle strained against muscle. A foot slipped, its owner losing his balance but determined to stay on top or take the other with him. A third dark shape joined the struggling knot of limbs, only to be sent sprawling. There was a pause, as both combatants ceased fighting to check that Tilana was safe, then immediately continued the contest. It was almost like farce – would have been had it not been enacted at such a great height.

Sharp sounds followed. The intensity of the battle increased. Yet they must have been tiring: hiding their fatigue from each other. Hairpulling. Gouging. Curses. They were getting desperate. They swayed dangerously near the edge.

I then realized something that made me panic. Somewhere up there was the ritual blade. One of the combatants would have it. Surely, there would be a death?

Suddenly, a sharp tremor went through the earth. The whole world shook for a brief moment and the vibrations travelled up the rock, making it quiver.

One of the figures seemed to detach itself from the pinnacle and took to the air like a juvenile bird, arms whirling in terror. There was a soft *thud*. The body lay at my feet.

To my relief I did not recognize him. I bent down and put my ear to his mouth. He still breathed. There was a thick layer of moss surrounding the rock, which its shadow and dripping water had fostered over the years. The sponginess had saved Tilana's brother. The next moment a rope struck my shoulder and I knew the other two were descending from their perch.

Immediately Tilana was on the ground she ran to her brother's prone body and carried out the same action as I had just performed. Then she turned to Clay.

'I'd never have forgiven you if you'd killed him.'

Clay dropped on one knee beside her to inspect the victim himself.

'Just stunned. He'll be all right.'

'He might have some broken bones,' said Tilana. 'I want to make sure. You go away. I'll see he's looked after.'

Clay gripped her wrist.

'No. You have to come with me. You belong to me . . . '

'I belong to *no one*,' she replied, fiercely.

'We belong together,' he countered, meekly.

I thought: I don't know where I belong, but I know where I'm going if I stay here.

'Look,' said Clay, echoing my thought, 'if we stay here we'll both die. I'm wanted by my Family for rejecting my mother. She killed herself. I did it for you. Surely you can do as much for me? Not kill him, but leave him. Come with me, *please*?'

'The vigil . . . My brother will hunt you down. Greatgramma – she'll be angry. Very angry. I don't know what to do.' She pulled at her hair in exasperation. 'What shall I *do*?'

'Come with me.'

'But – where will we go? There's nowhere we can hide forever. They'll find us in the end. And there'll be a war between the Families. A blood feud. All because of us. Why did you have to do this? You are a fool, Clay. You are . . . ' Her large eyes filled with tears and suddenly she fell on his shoulder and sobbed. He held her close, crooning softly in her ear. I could see the triumph in his features. He had her. He knew he had her.

'Where will it all end?' she groaned.

73

'In life,' Clay said promptly and with an edge to his voice. 'We'll find somewhere, you'll see. Already I've managed to evade my Family for several days. I found this place below a waterfall and have kept myself. I can keep you too. We don't need anyone else. Just us.'

He had kept himself? I had never needed gratitude but it would have been nice to have been acknowledged for something. Now it seemed I was to become keeper to two, instead of one.

'What about that?' she said, pointing to me. 'Do we have to look after that as well? Can't we get rid of it?'

This was too much. I felt the anger boiling over inside me. She was not part of my Family. She had no right to talk of me in that manner. I could keep silent no longer.

'Where my brother goes, I go. I may not speak to him, but you? I care nothing about you.'

She ignored me.

'Well?' she asked of Clay.

'I can't prevent my shadow from following me, any more than you can,' he said, staring at the trees. 'I don't want to fight over a shadow. It's best ignored.'

'Listen to him,' I said. 'We've been together all our lives. He knows what is right.'

Tilana snorted. 'Oh, yes. He knows what's right. A mother dead. A brother crippled. Two people banished. Clay knows what's right.'

'You had nothing to do with it I suppose,' I countered. 'He did it all alone.'

'Yes.' Then she turned away from me and I knew it was going to be all right. Never again did she suggest that 'it' should be disposed of, though there was always an antipathy between us. We tolerated each other because of Clay. She had the better of it because though she was never, to my knowledge, jealous of me, I am ashamed to say I resented her quite deeply.

Tilana's brother stirred and Clay pulled her away quickly. I realized he wanted to get her away before the youth came to and was able to speak. It was not beyond the bounds of possibility that Tilana could be persuaded not to go with Clay.

She protested, but weakly. I stumbled along beside them. I did not want to be around when the Night Family came and saw what had happened to the vigil.

74

A little while later the night was full of blood-chilling cries and I knew the hunt was on. Now we would be pursued by night *and* day, never given rest. How were we going to eat?

We found the stream to the waterfall and followed it down mid-water to hide our tracks. Once on the ledge Tilana lay down full length, but there was not enough room for all of us to do that, so Clay and I sat side by side, propped up against the rockface. The Deadplace yawned below us, full of its own terrors. At that moment I think I would have been prepared to face a ghoul rather than a human, however terrifying it was.

I spent the night listening to my friends the stones. From the other two came whispered recriminations and urgent protestations. All night long. When dawn came I was weary of both of them, but was aware of my responsibilities. I felt the need to look after these two children.

Later, I climbed up from the ledge to see if we were in any danger of being discovered. Even though it was well past dawn the trees had remained dark and strange, as if they still had the night tangled up in their branches and could not shake it loose. The clouds were a yellow ochre – the colour of leafsmoke. We were in for heavy rain and there would be mud in the drops as there sometimes was during the wet season. It was neither night nor day: a sort of in-between world which engendered weird movement – shadows darting from rock to rock, or gliding swiftly over the surface of the lake. I climbed back down to the ledge.

Tilana was saying to Clay, 'We can't stay here when the rain comes. If there's a flood we'll be washed off.' She looked exhausted. Around her eyes were dark rings and I could see that the light was bothering them. They watered incessantly. I was pleased for her that it was not full daylight.

Clay noticed too.

'Have you ever been out in the sunlight?'

He stroked her cheek as he spoke.

'Once or twice. I can't see very well and it's painful. It's as if a white haze has settled on the world. I can see shapes – blurred, bright phantoms – but I can't make out details.'

'We'll get you some palm gauze,' I said. 'To make a band for your eyes. You'll be able to see through it but the light won't be so strong.'

'If you like,' she said. 'What do you think, Clay?'

'Don't do that to him,' I cried. 'Don't make him acknowledge me. I don't want it. When he does, I'll know he doesn't love me any more. You don't understand us. There's never been any *unwanted* in your Family that have been allowed to live, have there?'

She shook her head. We both fell silent for a moment, then she said, 'Clay told me about you.' There was something about her tone I didn't like and I became aggressive.

'What? What did he tell you?'

'That you were found.'

'Found?' I was puzzled. 'Found where?'

'Just *found*.'

'That's not true. Catrunner was my mother.'

She smiled sweetly.

'How do you know?'

'Because ... because I know. A child knows its own mother.'

Inside me, my heart was pounding and I felt a great pain. An emotional pain. This creature was trying to tell me that Clay was not my brother. That Catrunner was not my parent did not affect me in the least, except that it would have severed my relationship with Clay if she were not. This girl was trying to destroy me. I began to hate her. I knew she was lying. She had to be. I could not have assumed Clay was my brother all these years and have been wrong.

'Why are you doing this to me?' I cried.

She turned to Clay.

'Isn't it true that your shadow was found for you?'

He turned, and glared at her so fiercely that she almost fell from the shelf in an effort to get away from him. Then a flush coloured her face. She looked suddenly ashamed.

'He said ... he said it was the younger sister. When she opened herself with the ritual stone ... '

She saw that I was confused, and said, 'You don't know all the ways of women.'

'I still don't understand.'

'It's the custom to do it on the Wedding Rock, before the new husband arrives. Your people do it too. So that the skin is broken gently, because a new husband is too eager, too rough ... ' She was blushing furiously by this time.

My mind was a whirl of weird images.

'What's all this got to do with me?'

'Your mother was a virgin – until she used the stone. Afterwards, the new husband was killed by a snake on his way to the wedding hut. Don't you understand. *She never lay with a man . . .* your mother was Catrunner's younger sister.'

'My mother was Catrunner,' I shouted. 'You're lying. You hate me, and that's why you're lying. You want to be Clay's sister and you're jealous of me . . .'

I felt like striking her, but all I did was clench my fists as her expressions ran a whole range of emotions, from triumph through to fear. Catrunner was my mother and that made Clay my brother. I didn't want to hear about any stupid sister. My whole body was trembling. I did not realize then, that what I was to become was far more important than my origins.

Tilana said, 'I'm sorry.' Her face was screwed up tight, but whether that was because of the light or some internal aggravation, I wasn't sure.

'It doesn't matter,' I said. But then I felt a need to explain. 'He knew that if he spoke to me, or if I spoke to him, they would kill me. I would have become real. He trained himself not to see me as I really am. Now he's been doing it for so long there's something inside his head that won't let him. A kind of blank spot. It's fixed in him, and I don't want him to change. I don't need him to talk to me. We get by fine without it. It would be uncomfortable. With you and me it's different. We didn't grow up together . . .'

'You didn't grow up at all,' she said abruptly, and turned her back on me.

Just then the first large drops of rain began to hit the rocks beside the waterfall. We started to climb up the slippery white slope to the top. The light faded rapidly and soon the rain was coming down almost as densely as the cataract.

We climbed to the top again and found a rock shelf nearby to shelter from the rain. Around the shelf there were huge cracks in the ground which drained the water swiftly from the surface. I sat and watched it gurgling down into the depths of the earth as the gloom around us found its way into my spirit. It was as if the murk had gathered and compressed itself into rock which pressed against my heart.

Then, as I sat staring at the muddy patterns in despondency, a shape suddenly formed in the wall of water before my eyes: a horrible, gnarled figure, bent and twisted like a tree that grows from the cavity in a rock. It moved towards us, leaning heavily on a crooked stick, water running from its form and obscuring the detail of its features. It grunted as it laboured over the mud, the sound of a pig giving birth, and each measured, slow step took it closer to our hiding place.

Clay let out a yell, which made me jump in fright. It was not a shout of fear – it was a warning to the creature to keep back. The figure paused, stooped and peered under the rock, into our eyes. She was so close I could smell the damp, soiled animal skin that she had draped over her head and shoulders to keep the rain off.

Tilana uttered one word.

'Greatgramma!'

Chapter Twelve

The old woman crawled under the rock shelf with us. Clay and I huddled in a space as far away from her as possible. She sat opposite Tilana and regarded her sorrowfully.

'Child, what have you done?' The Greatgrandmother of the Night Family nodded her head and in the silence I could hear the bones in her neck cracking with the movement.

'The whole Family are out looking for you, even in the day and the rain. Ruanna cries all the time. Why child? Why did you desert your brother Ruanna for these . . .' She gave Clay and me a look of disgust. Her creased little monkey's face with its huge moon eyes then turned again to Tilana and I could see the girl shaking, I supposed in fear.

'I'm sorry, Greatgramma. It . . . it just happened. Is he all right – Ruanna? He's not hurt is he?'

'Your brother has a broken leg, but he will live. It's you I'm concerned for. There will have to be punishment. Have you . . .?' She flicked a glance towards Clay.

'No, but I don't want to leave him, Greatgramma. Too much has happened now – in here,' she pointed to her own breast. 'I know it's wrong, but the wrong can't be put right now.'

'There are no such feelings outside *Family*.'

'But there *must* be, because I have them, for him. I want to be with him – all the time. I love my brother too, but it's different. Oh, you'll never understand. Nobody will.' The tears began welling up in her eyes. 'I can't help it. It's just *there*. It won't go away because I've tried. I've tried to destroy them, but they keep growing again, stronger.'

'You're wrong, child. I *do* understand,' said the brittle creature. 'But it's not to be.'

Tilana tilted her chin.

'Then we'll kill ourselves,' she said.

Her voice was firm and hard. I knew by the tone that she was not making a threat she did not intend to carry out. The Greatgrandmother looked thoughtful and a bleakness came over her.

'Child, child.'

'It's gone too far, Greatgramma. We can't go back now. I know I was your favourite – and I've disappointed you terribly. I'm sorry, but it was not in my will to do otherwise. If it had been, I would have done anything rather than hurt you, or Ruanna. Clay is – well, I don't care if our children are deformed – I want his babies. She . . .'Tilana pointed at me. 'Shadow is an *unwanted*, but lives.'

'Lives, yes. But *should* it? This whole thing is retribution from Redgod for allowing that thing to breathe longer than its first few seconds of life. *Evil*. See how ugly it is . . .'

I blurted out, 'Like you!'

The old woman grimaced. 'Not like me. My ugliness is the result of age, not birth. You have brought this sin upon us . . .'

'Don't blame me,' I countered. 'I tried to stop it.'

The rain thundered down around us, creating a backdrop of noise to the argument. The shrivelled old woman's eyes bore into my own.

'You tried to stop it,' she repeated, slowly. She turned again to Tilana. 'I do understand this *love* you speak of – but it comes from the Deadplace, not Redgod. This creature has brought something with it from that land and planted it in your hearts. It's . . .'

'I've never been to the Deadlands. *Never* . . .' I shouted.

The Greatgrandmother ignored me.

She said, 'There must be punishment to exorcise the evil. You, child, and this boy are not to blame. It is *that*,' she pointed to me without looking at me, 'which is to blame. If we were to make a sacrifice – Redgod would be appeased. Burn it, and this *feeling*, this cankerous thing that is rotting, festering in your hearts, will disappear. You will be clean. Burn the beast and there need be no more punishment. I am sure the Day Greatgrandmother would agree – and the Families, having been told by us how you were bewitched, would be forgiving . . .'

Tilana looked at Clay quickly. My brother picked up a rock from the ground.

'No,' he said, emphatically.

The old woman smiled, cavernously.

'Ah – this *good* love would have you kill me, eh?'

Tilana shook her head. 'Clay, put down the stone.' She turned to the Greatgramma. 'We've made our decision. There's no going back. Clay's mother is dead. The death was an accident, but we can't bring her back to life. Clay's Family will persecute him, whatever you say. And I don't want to live without him.'

The old woman sat, regarding the three of us for a long time, then let out a huge sigh. Her whole frame shuddered with the exhalation, as if her heart were broken.

'I see there is no way to put things right. This love of yours comes from the Deadplace – you must take it to where it belongs. The three of you must leave here and go to join the devils which have called for you. If you stayed and were found, the effect on the Families – no, it's best you disappear without trace . . .'

'But how . . .?' said Tilana.

'There is a way. See how the rain falls through the cracks in the ground? There is a place where the cracks are so wide a person can climb down into the earth. Passages. I am told they lead to the Deadlands. Of course, I cannot be sure, but you have no choice. These secrets passed down from one Greatgramma to another are old – they are said to be the truth, but I have learned to trust nothing in my long life. Especially words. And when you get there, you will have the Deadlands and their ghosts to contend with . . .' She paused, then added. 'It is all I can offer.'

I thought: this is the rainy season. Perhaps the old witch was trying to get us to enter the tunnels so that we would be drowned? The rain would flood the passages and we would be trapped.

But there were two arguments that made me reject this potential betrayal. The first was that no matter what she did, the Greatgramma could not command the rain to fall when she pleased. There would be no guarantee of that happening while we were descending. Secondly, why? Surely, if she believed we were destined for the Deadplace, there would be no need to kill us. That destination was more terrifying than death itself.

Tilana said, 'Never. I'll never go down there.'

'Nor me,' confirmed Clay.

'You have no choice,' repeated the hag. 'Listen to me, child. If you remain, the youngsters will see you die declaring your – attachment to each other. We cannot allow that, for they would

81

soon begin to question *Tilana* and *Clay* in their minds, and we cannot allow any doubt. Whether you go of your own free will now, or force us to do it for you, your destination is the Deadland below. Walk there or be thrown.

'Yes, you were my favourite. Yours is the mind of an eagle – it soars beyond this Cloudrock of ours. All you wanted was one small chance to be different from the others – and you took it. I have watched you grow – seen the restlessness growing in you. Now you have to take the consequences. The Deadplace may not be as bad as we fear. Or it might be worse. Who can know? You must find out.'

The Greatgrandmother smiled wanly, then her thin arm flashed out and her hand gripped Tilana's wrist.

'When the rain stops, we will go to the place.'

Tilana said bitterly, 'Never to return. We *mustn't* corrupt the young, must we?'

Some time later the rain stopped and the old woman motioned for us to follow her. We were about to leave when Clay gave a loud shout. When I turned to look at him his appearance shocked me. His eyes looked abnormally bright and feverish, and there was a glistening to his brow.

'Quickly,' he cried in a shrill voice. 'We've got to go down – down to the Deadplace. I'm not afraid. Where's my weapon, my bow? I haven't got it. I must find a new one. A spear. Yes, a spear. Don't worry, I'll protect us. Which is the way? Show us the way. We have to go down. I must find a spear . . .'

He jumped up and began to pace backwards and forwards. The bent, crooked form of the Greatgrandmother moved off and Tilana followed. I took Clay's hand and led him after them. He was still muttering, 'A spear – a spear . . .' but made no attempt to find a suitable stave amongst the broken trees that we passed. Finally, Tilana stooped amongst some bushes, having found a straight sapling that was easy to uproot, and thrust it into Clay's hand. He clutched at it as if it were the answer to all our problems. As if now that he had his 'spear' no harm could come to us. It was his talisman, to ward off all evil.

The hag led us inland and I began to suspect a trap – though what could be worse than that to which she was sending us I had no idea. Eventually, however, we came to a place where there were some caves.

'You will need torches,' said the old woman. 'Tilana . . . there is dry wood in that cave. Find it and make several brands. You, the ugly one – make fire. The boy is useless for anything at the moment. I hope for your sake child, that he recovers his wits quickly.'

I did as I was told, making a bow drill and finding dry grass just inside the cave. Soon I had a flame and we lit three brushwood brands which Tilana had prepared. We stuck spare torches in our waistbands. Clay had been busily sharpening a point on his spear with an edged stone.

Tight-lipped, and a little pale now, Tilana asked the Great-grandmother where the holes were, down which we were to descend.

'At the rear of the cave, child.' A shadow crossed the old woman's face. 'Goodbye, child. Don't come back. You have made your choice, now you must see it through.'

They touched foreheads.

'Tell Ruanna . . .' began Tilana, but the woman interrupted her.

'I shall tell him nothing. You are gone from us. He must marry your younger sister and forget all about you.'

A look of pain passed over Tilana's face. She nodded.

'Now go.'

The last words of her Greatgramma. We left the strange creature standing with the light behind her in the cave doorway, hunched, black, sinister. Light scattered from around her. A dark kernel, shrivelled. What demons could we meet worse than that sight? None. A body shrinking to baby-size. And ugly. More deformed than the worst of the *unwanted*. Yet, she lived. Lived and enjoyed respect. The highest respect. *Old woman, old woman, you perpetrate wrong*. And if she were wrong, we were right. My last look. The light seemed to close in around her. She was frail. Frail as a cobweb. Perhaps soon the light would be too much? It would crush her skull. So fragile, so flimsy, that even light will crush. Yet strong enough to destroy us. Strong, enough. Enough.

Clay led the way into the cave, followed by Tilana, and then me. We found the chimney and began to climb down by pressing with outstretched limbs against its walls. It was wet and slippery but the sloping shelves of rock allowed us to grip with our feet while using our hands to balance. The smoke from the flickering torches was swept quickly upwards by a strong draught of air coming from below and I, being the last in the chain, was having difficulty breathing. The fumes got in my nostrils and eyes, making the latter smart with pain. It was something I had to endure however and it was useless to complain. We needed light.

The blackness was utter and made the descent slow and arduous. Very soon my arms and legs were aching through having to employ normally unused muscles. There was an anxiousness between us, almost like a line, knitting our bodies together. We moved with a kind of controlled urgency, desperate to be outside once more – even though it would be the Deadplace – but knowing that we had to climb down carefully to avoid injuries.

The air became stifling and the darkness did not bear contemplation – it was as dense as liquid and flowed around us. Within our small bubble of light we were safe from its suffocating waves, but if our torches failed ... we would drown in blackness. Of course, Tilana's eyes were used to darkness, so she was less inclined to be afraid, but the impenetrable black of this underground kingdom of the night was quite different from the one she was used to above ground. If we lost the torchlight, she would become just as blind as Clay and me. Anyway, it was not *just* the dark. It was also the feeling of being locked in, with rock on all sides, over and below us, because the peculiar zig-zagging of the chimney meant that there was always a ceiling and floor as well as walls. Still, she was used to caves and darkness of a kind and could see better than either Clay or myself and was therefore relatively less insecure in her movements.

The rock and coral too, seemed alive and viscous to the sight. Of course, when we touched it, it was solid enough, though running with surface water, but in the dancing torchlight it seemed to warp and ripple, and there were changing faces in its aspect. Eyes, long and hollow, and drawn mouths, appeared for an instant to haunt me. The mouths opened occasionally, as if to swallow my hand as I placed it against some ghoulish feature, and once or twice I withdrew it involuntarily in case it was severed at the wrist. Those faces in the rock were mocking spirits

84

that surfaced at our approach and watched with amused contempt our progress down the shaft.

I had never before been afraid of rocks and stones but this place seemed like an otherworld of their kind: a prison to which evil rocks were sent to fester into ugly shapes and growths. It was the Deadplace of stonekind. I could not commune with them. They were as far away from me as the Family.

Once, I shouted, 'Go away! Go away!' and the echoing yell startled my two companions into terrible screams of fear, until we were all screaming hysterically at one another, and at nothing at all. It was some time before our voices gave out and the noise subsided.

We crouched on individual shelves, trembling in terror for a long time, each afraid to move in case one of us started screaming again and recreated that terrible spiral of mounting sound and fear. During the silence that followed I heard Clay whimper once or twice in a tiny voice. The thin sounds were cut off abruptly, however, as if he had just realized that it was him making the noise and not wanting to recall the demons had stemmed the whimpers the instant he knew they were coming from his own mouth. He clutched the stick he carried as if it were some magic talisman. It was no longer a spear: it was a thing of power from the live world outside that could ward off evil. It came from green, living trees and contact with it gave my brother strength in this place of hollow madness.

Eventually, as we continued the descent, the torches began to flicker more furiously and I could feel a strong wind on my face.

'We must be near the outside,' I whispered to Tilana. 'Can you feel the air?'

'I can *feel* it,' she replied in a dubious tone, 'but I can't *smell* it. It has no scent.'

She was right. The draught had that same musty odour which had been our companion since we had entered the hole. I wondered whether this was indeed the scent of the Deadworld, this single smell which failed to enliven the senses in any way whatsoever. It was dull and heavy and full of oppression.

Just then the narrow passage opened up and after clambering over some loose rocks a rushing sound hit our ears. We looked at one another fearfully but there was no option but to continue with the journey. We climbed out into a huge void.

We found ourselves waist-deep in water. It was bitterly cold.

'It's not like the colour of the lake,' I heard Clay mutter. He was right. It was green, not blue. A kind of clean greenness that I had never seen before. It was the walls of the chamber which were blue – but not the blueness of sky: more the dull blue of metal in certain light. Here and there were patches of dark yellow, like sores on the main body, which stood proud of the glistening rockface.

Standing in the stream we lit new torches and raised them to see if we could find the ceiling but the walls of rock went vertically upwards into the magical darkness. They seemed to go on forever. I no longer felt enclosed. I now had the sense of too much space. I was as small as a beetle in this hollow place of echoes and shadows, where the only sounds were the muted dongs of distant, falling stones striking bells of rock, and the steady rain on the surface of the water. Our own movements seemed a disturbing, unwelcome invasion of someone's privacy: someone unseen but whose shallow breathing could be heard in the blackness above.

In the blue moonlight cast by the reflected torches we proceeded along the green river. The rock was sharp and we had to tread warily. We passed through passages of blackrock needles which all pointed in one direction. We crossed chambers where clusters of scallop-shaped stones were piled one on the other, making beautiful cascades. We drank from raised basins into which water dripped continually. We passed beneath stone trees whose branches were lost in the darkness above. Once we passed below an enormous wing-shaped canopy. Everything we saw was fashioned for the use of giants. Though we were weary, and half cold in the water, we pressed on quickly with this thought in mind.

Sounds bounced around us. We grew very tired. The journey seemed endless. My body screamed at me to stop but my mind was stronger. I would *not* fall. Would *not*. Drips and splash sounds folded over and over on themselves until they eventually swallowed each other.

Several times during our journey we came to a point where we had to make a decision, being faced with a choice of passages. Each time I seemed to know instinctively which one to take but at first Tilana tried to assert her authority.

'Not that way, Shadow. The breeze is strongest here. I can feel it on my cheek.'

Clay would have a different opinion but would not state his case emphatically, and merely muttered, 'I think we should go down here.'

'You're wrong,' I would argue. 'This narrow one is the passage that leads to the outside.'

'You think that's the way to go?'

'I'm sure it is.'

But we would usually end up following Tilana's lead and inevitably find that the passage was a dead end. The trouble was, she would choose the most accessible-looking passage and the one down which the path actually lay was often the most forbidding at the outset. I would have to lead them back to the point where we had made our choice. When this had happened two or three times, Tilana gave up her leadership to me and I merely indicated which way we should go.

I did not know, then, why my instincts were always correct, though I did feel that it was something to do with the closeness I had always had with the earth and rocks. I felt their rhythms, their tides, running through me at all times and when there was a question between us I knew when the rhythms were right, and when they were wrong.

Tilana made one last bid at a point where there was only a choice between two. She turned out to be right – but what I did not tell her was that either passage would have led us to the outside, for they joined together later.

After travelling for many, many rods we came to a cavern which seemed bottomless. I threw a stone into the space and though I heard it striking the walls in its descent, I could not be sure I heard it hit the bottom. We found a series of ledges around this pit and then a dry chamber beyond, the stream having to throw itself in the depths of the hole we had skirted – a fate I did not envy our erstwhile companion in the least.

High above us, in this new hall of splendour, was a hole through which the daylight poured. It was as far away from us as earth is from the sun and in no way accessible, but it showed us yet another strange world. We stood, shivering off the affects of the coldwater stream, and stared about us in wonder, at the cones of stone like the elongated homes of termites reaching higher than the tallest tree I had ever seen. Mirror images of these giants threatened to fall from the ceiling and spear us where we stood. There were fluted formations – enormous fans which spread across an area the size of our old village and great arches which seemed to shoulder the weight of the walls that pressed inwards.

We passed through this hall in awe, and following the passage with the strongest draught, continued our walk through the stomach of the world. The wildlife suddenly made itself apparent at this point. The place was full of swift birds which flew with arrowfast speed through the light of our brands and there were many striped snakes wrapped around the stems of rocks.

Once, Tilana shouted, 'Look out, Shadow,' just as one of these slim creatures struck close to my head. But there had been no danger. It had snatched one of the small birds out of the air near to my face. The birds were swift but the snakes were quicker.

The sound of the birds' high-pitched cries always preceded and fell in behind us. As soon as they came into the light of the torches they ceased their calling. Underneath our feet was a soft layer of excrement in which were many other kinds of creatures: spiders, worms and insects of all kinds. All this animal life existed in total darkness.

At long last we came to a point where the wildlife was joined by vegetation: lichen covered the surfaces of the rocks. We had to swim across a pool at this stage and on the other side, within the space of ten paces, all senses suddenly changed. The smell of the jungle swamped us with all its accompanying sensations. Perspectives narrowed with the gradually lowering ceiling and we could hear the sounds of the outside invading the inner world. After being deprived of these sensations for what was perhaps almost a day they broke over us like a flood and my whole body suddenly pricked with life and new energy. I was no longer weary to the point of death – I was merely tired and full of optimism. I felt as if I were floating on a warm current of air. Huge moths brushed my face as I walked and I delighted in their contact. Tilana and Clay were talking animatedly to one another. None of us, at that point, remembered that our destination was the Deadplace and that we were not passing from one highplace to another, similar environment, because our senses told us differently. The feeling did not last long.

'I think we should rest here,' said Tilana, 'before . . .' She left the rest unsaid and we were all plunged instantly into gloomy foreboding. Those few words had opened our future to us again. We recalled where we were going. We moved closer together for comfort and anxiety re-established itself within, all the more determined since it had been denied its place of residence for a brief period.

I tried to visualise what the scene would be like outside. Were those smells, those sounds, mere trickery on the part of the ghouls which we knew were waiting for us? All I could picture was a misty region which fell away below me and beyond this a dead flatland. We had been in the womb of Cloudrock and were about to be reborn, but into what kind of world?

I could hear Clay striking the rock ahead of me as we walked towards a narrow slit of light and I wondered whether he was doing it out of anger or impatience . . . or just absently hitting out, finding courage in the sound, a kind of comfort. It was as if he were drumming us out into our new life, marking the separation from the old one.

We moved slower and slower as we approached the white, blinding seam until, eventually, we stopped.

I curled up on a rock immediately, my eyes towards that uninviting slit ahead. Clay and Tilana lay wrapped in each other's arms behind me. Shortly afterwards I heard them moving against each other.

Not now! I thought. This is not the time to break the cycle!

But they did what they had to do. If it had been me I would have waited until the old world was firmly behind us and new horizons were within reach. There seemed to be something terribly wrong about breaking a taboo within the sacred confines of the Family temple. I can only equate it to seizing a stool shortly after the owner's death and chopping it up to use as firewood within sight of the holy log.

It was both blasphemous and sinful. Such behaviour was unworthy of both of them. Yet, I also realized that they needed to join in more than spirit before facing the dangers, natural and otherwise, of the Deadplace beyond that crack of light. They had to create a union, a togetherness, which would give them the strength they needed to face the outside. (Also, now, I have to admit I was more than a little jealous. Someone had replaced me in my brother's arms. Someone who could give him more than the love of kin. I could no longer crawl to his side and imbibe comfort from his warm presence. Tilana had taken my place.)

The last thing I remembered, before falling asleep, was that I had left my little stool behind.

I awoke once, probably just a short time afterwards. It was coming on nightfall and I experienced a few moments of high panic. There was a rustling sound in the air as if someone were running over dead, crisp palm leaves. I raised myself on one elbow and stared at the other two in the poor light, but they were fast asleep, locked in one another's bodies. The noise increased in volume. It seemed to be coming from somewhere above.

Just at that moment the sun had dropped low enough on the horizon to shine directly into the cave and looking up it appeared that the ceiling was alive, rippling with dark waves. Just as I was about to call out to Clay, the whole roof of the cave seemed to detach itself and broke up into thousands of pieces of flapping fabric. The noise, though soft, carried far back into the cave and resembled the sound of heavy raindrops hitting waxy leaves on the roof of a forest.

Bats! They were only bats. They funnelled through the opening – the width of a man – and out into the night regions. By the time the last one had left it was pitch black outside and, feeling uneasy, I rose and put my arm through the narrow gap to reassure myself that it was not blocked. Why, I do not know, except that I had been robbed of light for so long I was beginning to form the irrational idea that someone was going to seal us in the darkness forever.

Finally, I lay back down on the rock floor and fell asleep. The returning night hunters fluttering back to their roosts would wake me in the morning.

Chapter Thirteen

I dreamed.

There was a rock in the forest, green with soft moss and lichen, on which a shaft of light shone. The trees stood around the rock as tall sentinels, guarding their charge. Warmth from the sun's javelin buried in its heart permeated every pore of the stone and it began to stir to life, taking on movement and forming the shape of a living creature, a child.

It stood up, on two small legs and uttered a sound, a cry, before taking its first few steps towards the edge of the forest, leaving its birthplace, its depression in the earth. On the edge of the woodland it stopped and surveyed a village of humans nearby: saw the children playing on the hard, packed earth: running, squealing, touching. Eagerly, it went to join them, to take part in these delightful games.

But the children saw it coming and knew it was a rock in human form. They scattered, screaming, running for the safety of adults in the yurts. The adults came and beat the newly born with sticks, driving it away to where it had come from. Yet, it was no longer a rock, it was a human and it tried to return, again and again, only to be driven back. It grew hungry and attempted to pick up the bones that were thrown away from the human's fireplace, but the other children, no longer afraid of it, snatched the bones from its hands just as it was raising the food to its mouth. They followed after it, jeering and screeching, never letting it rest, throwing clods of earth at it when it tried to sleep and driving it away from the water when it tried to drink.

The rockchild was full of misery. Only one of the children showed any kindness to it at all and it did that by completely ignoring it, allowing it to trail around after him unmolested, even allowing it to pick fruit from the orchard and fill its belly without hindrance. Gradually, the others began to leave it alone and only when the kind one was not in sight did they occasionally throw a stone or push it sprawling in the mud.

It grew, seeking solace amongst its own kind, the rocks and stones, and dreaming of a time when it would be free of the place on which it was born.

I awoke.

Chapter Fourteen

There was daylight outside.

I could hear the noises of forest creatures: the parrots calling to one another, the sound of mammals marking out their territories. Wildlife, and the background of hissing waterfalls. It did not sound any different from the world above. I went to the blinding-white crack and peered out. I could smell vegetation.

Jungle.

Cautiously, I squeezed through the gap. Once outside, I crouched instinctively, ready to run back inside the cavern should I be attacked. A parakeet screeched and I half-turned but stayed, shaking a little. This place was strange to me – yet familiar. I recognized nothing, but at the same time there was little difference between this environment and the one I had left. A little more lush perhaps, but certainly no more sinister.

It was high up, a jungled slope that swept downwards in a curve and melted into the mists below. Above my head was the white underside of Cloudrock, its broad brim reaching out some distance from where I stood. From its edge fell the waterfalls in torrents of spray which dazzled with colours in the sunlight. Quite beautiful. Not at all frightening. The air was cool, sparkling, though damp and difficult to breathe. It clung to my eyebrows and hair, and was soon running in rivulets down my face and back.

A world of rainbows.

I stood there for a long time, watching the bright twists of water roping their way downwards, to fray into wild ends. Now and then I would catch sight of a bird in the foliage, or a small mammal, curious about this new visitor to its world, parting the leaves with a sharp nose, its glittering eyes intent upon my face.

From the top of Cloudrock this world was not visible.

So, there was game and fruit here. We would not starve,

neither would we thirst. Why, we could live here forever and not worry about the world above us!

I went inside again and woke the other two. They were as astonished as I had been and clung to each other, laughing like small children.

The first thing we did was to fit Tilana out with some protection for her shoulders and eyes, using palm trunk gauze. Then we set about gathering food, for we were extremely hungry. In the forest it was dark and we became a little wary once more, our heads full of old stories of ghosts. They said you could smell a phantom approaching – a stink like no other odour – and we crept along through the undergrowth sniffing furtively at the small clearings and jumping at any sound we had not been expecting. The curiosity of the human is indomitable however, and though we were frightened at times we managed to explore the whole of the upper slope for fifty rods on either side, during the first day.

On the first night we returned to the cave to sleep because the damp air was an uncomfortable blanket. On the second day we set off down the slope to the water at the bottom, battling our way through clouds of fine spray. The drifting mists were a constant source of irritation to us, since we were never able to dry off completely and there was hope among us that there would be a place beyond the foot of the slope which was free of the damp.

There was a curious unease setting in between Tilana and Clay, which I too experienced. I felt sure that this was because we were now definitely cut off from the mainstream of the Family. Cut off from the life-force by a roof of rock. Tilana said she was afraid our blood would stagnate like a backwater. It would grow dark and sluggish. Eventually, she said, we would be carrying it around like useless weight, a dead fluid. Now, I realize that what we were feeling was merely homesickness, but at the time it seemed like a physical malady.

When we reached the outer rim, right beneath the waterfalls, Tilana suddenly stopped and pointed dramatically.

'What are they?'

In the trees and scattered round us on the ground were many white skeletons glistening with water. Several of the limbs were missing or parted from the main collection of bones. Most of the skeletons were small, shining pathetic heaps, but occasionally there was a larger one. Deformities were evident in many of the bones which dangled, caught in the foliage above our heads, or lay sprawled on some rocky patch where the vegetation had been denied access.

Little white skulls stared in all directions through hollow eye-sockets. Even the most recent bones had been picked clean by birds and animals and given a final polish by the ants. Caught in their angular gestures they seemed to be appealing to some deity who was everywhere, yet nowhere, for justice. Bony hands still reached out, grasping for some invisible handhold, failing to arrest that last terrifying fall through blackness. For most of them the fall had been their first, as well as their last, their *only* experience, of the world of mortals.

The graveyard of the *unwanted*.

'You know what they are,' I told Tilana. 'This is where I would have been if Clay hadn't looked after me.'

She showed no remorse and Clay, after turning over a couple of the nearest skeletons with his foot, lost interest. They both walked off, to some other part of the forest, leaving me to myself and my kin for a while. I gathered those on the ground and laid them out in a long neat row, staring up at their murderers with those black, accusing sockets. Those at the top of trees I left. There they rested, some of them only in part, like white birds nesting their young for eternity. The thunder of the waterfalls their never-ending shout of anger. The swirling mists their spirits in turmoil.

Just beyond the foot of the slope was a narrow but deep trench, wherein the spilled water from Cloudrock ran, then issued forth as clouds of hot steam. I dropped a coconut into this crack in the Deadworld and failed to hear it strike the bottom.

On the other side of this trench was a desert of glistening crystals: a wide, white stretch broken only by an occasional island of coarse green vegetation. It was a salt flat – a hollow world where nothing seemed to move except wraith-like mists curling between its oases. Forbidding, yet at the same time it had a magnetic quality, drawing my soul from my body. Though it appeared to invite the tread of human feet the prospect of going out there was frightening.

The first night out in the rain forest had been a traumatic experience in itself, with our ears constantly tuned for the sound of a stranger's footsteps and our bodies tense and ready for flight. Even during the day, there had been a vestige of apprehension threading us together, so that we never moved far from one another.

None of us got much sleep during that first night – Tilana especially, since she had to adjust to different hours. We lay in a nest we had formed for ourselves at the base of three trees and the other two whispered to each other occasionally when they needed the comfort of a voice. The constant roar of the waterfalls sent vibrations through my body which helped me rather than disturbed me. I felt a sense of peace in the earth, spiritual peace, which seemed to belie any horrors which infested the world around us. No phantoms came.

Living in the rain forest was not at all pleasant. We began to develop chills and coughs as the fine wet air invaded our lungs. Our skins began to wrinkle and pucker through constant exposure to moisture. The whole time it was uncomfortable: not just an irritating but a miserable existence. Clay and Tilana grew more morose as the days passed. They sat huddled together like two babes, time on time, staring back up at the world from which we had descended. There was rain inside, as well as outside them.

I too felt the tug of the invisible fisherman's line from above, but not as badly as the other two. I guessed they would snap that line soon and left them to their yearning, taking the time to do a little more exploring on my own. The pull from those salt wastes was just as strong to me as the call for them from Cloudrock. I waited for my companions to harden.

I began venturing out of the rain forest onto the flats. There were several places along the chasm where it narrowed some few rods below the edge and I had to climb down with a vine, using small handholds, into the suffocating abyss to a point where I could reach across and ascend the other side. Though I knew that neither of the other two would have done the same I felt no great pride because I felt no fear. I knew instinctively that the earth would not let me fall into its stomach. I was able to string a vine bridge between the two vertical walls for the time when the other two would need to cross with me. Once this had been done I actually enjoyed crossing the gap. I had steam baths as I monkeyed along the bridge. This vapour came out as irregular exhalations, as though the earth were some firebreathing monster, huffing through half-closed lips.

There was not a great deal out on the wastes, of course: a little life in the spongy greenness of the oases but only the occasional snake, bird or lizard. Enough life to support a group of three nomadic humans. Life feeding on life. The cyclic process. All the while I kept a wary eye on the wastes for the sight and sound of ogres, but saw nothing.

'Where do you keep disappearing to?' asked Tilana one day.

'Out there,' I replied, pointing.

'Why?'

'Because it's warm and dry and I hate being wet all the time. I can't breathe in this place. My insides are full of water . . .'

During such exchanges between Tilana and myself, Clay always averted his head, as if Tilana were talking to herself like some crazy-woman. My brother was an active youth and I knew that he was becoming restless. He constantly paced back and forth, threw himself on his back, stared at the sky, jumped up, began pacing again. Tilana too, was becoming edgy, though she showed it in different ways. She made weapons for the two of them: spears with stone tips, spending painstaking hours getting the balance right and testing the flight path of the shafts.

She said, 'There's nothing out there,'

'And there's nothing in here,' I answered.

The Greatgramma had indicated that the wanderlust was in Tilana and I wanted to nurture this trait until it became a goad.

'There's something out there Tilana. I can hear it's voice inside me . . . calling me. It tells me to come to it.'

I wanted to tell her about the sounding of the stars at night. How they jangled a rhythm in my head which said, 'Walk, Shadow, walk. See the white horizons full of promise? Hear the distant moon, crooning its seductive song? It says, walk, walk, walk . . .'

I wanted to tell her about the silent voices that spoke to my heart. The voices of wind and water, of sunlight and shade. Each stone, each rock, whispered, 'Go.' The distant wasteland, glinting with a million tiny crystals of whitefire called, 'Come.' How could I ignore these voices?

I wanted to tell her, but at the time I did not have the language, I did not own the words. They were just intrusive strangers in my head, wayward passions in my breast. She would not have understood such vague communications. All she could hear was that one single voice from her homeland, urging her to return to her cave, her people, her family.

How can you put into words the unified voice of the earth and sky, that cries from stone to stone, that rings from star to star, to someone whose only inner sound is the rush and gush of blood? I had to teach her to look out, not in.

Chapter Fifteen

I should have guessed that Clay and Tilana did not have the courage to cross the Deadplace. I awoke one morning to find that they had gone. I was alone again. They had failed me. Or had I somehow failed them? I was as confused as I had ever been.

I had no doubts as to *where* they had gone. There was only one place to go, apart from out into the wasteland: back to the top of Cloudrock.

I stared up at my old country with a feeling of resignation in my breast. Where my brother had gone, I would have to go too. We were inseparable. But I decided to give myself one more day of freedom. One more day of life, before retracing my steps through the underground caverns to an almost certain execution.

So, I wandered through the damp forest, visiting the place where the skeletons of the *unwanted* were decorating the trees. Then, towards evening, I made a small fire in the entrance to the cave and lit a torch. Just as the dusk came in and Redgod's presence filled the sky, I began the journey back to the top.

Once inside the body of the earth, I allowed my instincts to direct me along the right passages and eventually I arrived back in the cave on Cloudrock. They were waiting for me: Yellowbark and the others. She gave out a shriek of triumph and dragged me by the hair all the way back to the yurts where I was placed under guard. I passed the night in misery, calling for my brother. He never came. Perhaps they had already killed him? I had no way of knowing.

The following morning, Yellowbark came to me. Her animosity had in no way been softened by the fact that she had me in her power again. Her hard eyes looked at me in scorn as she sat down in front of me in the gloom of the yurt.

'Well, little hunchback, you thought you'd escaped my wrath, eh?'

'Where's Clay?' I asked. 'Let me see him.'

She spat contemptuously.

'There's been some changes around here, since I took over,' she said. 'And there'll be a few more.' She ran her stumpy fingers through her hair. 'However, you'll be pleased to hear that I don't intend to execute your brother. The Greatgrandmother of the Night Family has been told by Redgod that a new family must be started . . .'

My misery was suddenly replaced by joy. They were going to let Tilana and Clay live! A new family. I listened to how that sticklimbed old Greatgramma had convinced both the Families that they had grown too large and that a split was necessary. Clay and Tilana were to move to the other side of Cloudrock.

Then came the catch. I saw Yellowbark smile.

'Of course, they cannot be allowed to remain as man and wife. Tilana will marry her brother. Clay will marry my daughter, Fantail. The four of them will be the heads of the new family. The law must be upheld.'

'And what about me?' I asked, quietly.

'You will go the way your mother should have sent you long ago,' she said.

I nodded. So, having climbed all the way back up to the top, they were going to throw me down again, into the rainforest. Only, this time, it was for good.

'It all worked out well for you, you old witch.'

Her eyes narrowed.

'I suppose you think you can call me names, now that you know you're going to die. Be careful. I can starve you to death, just as easily, and that would be a painful way to go, dwarf. Better to fly into the arms of death, than to drip away, in agony.'

She reminded me that I was hungry.

'Can I have some food now,' I asked, 'or are you going to get rid of me straight away?'

'Tonight will see you flapping your arms over the edge of Cloudrock.'

She left the yurt and I quickly searched inside the pot on the hearth. There was a nice bone, still meaty.

It was the smoked remains of a human arm. I grabbed it and began tearing the crisp meat from the bone. Someone had already eaten the soft, fleshy parts and only the tough muscle remained, but that did not bother me. I was used to leftovers. Yellowbark returned, saw me eating, and looked very shocked. Suddenly she smiled.

'Who is it?' I asked, with my mouth full.

Yellowbark laughed.

'Your mother – so called – who else would it be?'

I tore another strip from the knuckle of a finger. My mother tasted good. I could have eaten her all day.

'I thought it might be Quickhand. I wouldn't want to eat someone I had killed. It wouldn't seem right.'

Yellowbark's eyes narrowed.

'Yes, you did that, didn't you? Well, all debts will be paid this evening . . .'

There was a commotion outside, just at that point, and suddenly someone burst into the yurt.

It was Tilana.

She glared at me.

'What did you have to come back for, you fool, Shadow? Why couldn't you stay where you were? We have to start a new life – but you?'

She turned to Yellowbark.

'Does the Shadow have to die?'

Yellowbark said, 'If I had my way, you'd be with him. You can thank your Greatgramma that you're not.'

'Why is he all covered in scratches?'

I looked down at my body. In my misery I had forgotten my wounds. I was covered in dried blood.

I said, 'She dragged me from the cave. It's all right. They don't hurt. And anyway, it's not going to matter much soon, is it? How's my brother?'

'Sick to his stomach that he's got to marry an ugly cousin, instead of me, but he doesn't know you've come back. We'll keep it from him until after . . . after . . .'

'After I jump.'

Her big eyes opened wide.

'You're going to jump?'

'Better than being thrown. Now, if you all don't mind, I wish to be alone with my mother,' I waved the arm in my hand, 'as we have some important things to do. I'm sure you understand.'

Yellowbark was still glaring at Tilana.

'My daughter is not ugly,' she said.

'Not compared to you,' said the tall, handsome girl, 'but to me . . .' With that she flounced out of the yurt. Yellowbark followed, almost immediately afterwards, leaving me in peace. Nothing had changed. They were still all at each other's throats.

I began chewing my mother's thumb, working my way through the fingers. If I was not mistaken, this was the arm that had reached out for me on its death-bed, and was hastily retrieved when its owner realized not *who*, but *what* I was. These were the fingers that had prised my own from the edge of her canoe, and set me adrift from her, when I needed her most. I had needed my mother to recognize me as her own child, but even at her last breath she could not bring herself to do that.

Ghastly woman. Tasted good though. I had come from inside her. Now she was going inside me. That was fair enough. Maybe one day I might find out that I was more of a woman, than a man, and have children of my own. Then I would see her again, in the faces of others . . .

I was dreaming. They were going to kill me in a little while. In no way was I part of the cycle of blood.

They came for me when the frogs began burping out their night cries. There was Yellowbark and two others: Vane and Anabla. Vane was of the Day Family and Anabla of the Night Hunters. Both families wanted to be sure that they had got rid of the nuisance.

I walked between them, keeping my silence. My legs were weak with fear, but I did not want to show it to these people. I could hear the rocks whispering to each other as I passed, and the trees moaning in the night wind. They knew I was going to die, but they could do nothing to save me.

The moon was big and yellow, filling her proportion of the sky. I intended to jump out at her. Try to leap the gap between us. It helped me to think I might make it. That I might land on her golden dust. Who would laugh then? Me.

We reached the edge of the cliff.

I walked out onto the small, natural platform that overhung the drop. My heart was pounding in my chest and it was all I could do to stop from turning around and running back into Yellowbark's arms, to beg for my life. But that would never have been granted and I wasn't going to give her the satisfaction.

'Goodbye, you old hag,' I said, without looking round. I hoped my voice did not betray my terror. There was no answer from behind me, so I took one more step forward, stretched my arms, and threw myself out into the blackness. I bit my tongue to stop myself from screaming. It was a brief, but glorious flight.

The landing was soft and springy. I bounced up into the air several times and then finally came to rest.

For a moment I just lay there, unable to believe that I was not a crumpled heap of bones and flesh. Then I heard voices, coming from the trees around me. Figures began scrambling around below me.

'Who's there?' I called, a new fear having taken place of the old one.

After all, this was the land of ghouls.

Chapter Sixteen

Hands pulled me from the place where I had landed and I found myself surrounded by a ring of faces which were only just visible in the moonlight. I could see eyes glinting and could hear the muttering of low voices.

'Don't frighten him,' cried one of them.

'I'm not a him – I'm an it,' I said, unable to think of anything else.

A female voice said, 'An adolescent. They kept this one a long time before throwing him over.'

'It,' I insisted. 'Throwing *it* over.'

There was a hand on my arm and I was guided through the crowd to a place where a fire was burning beneath a huge canopy. Once there, I saw in the firelight that the person with me was an elderly woman with white hair.

'I thought you might be ghosts,' I gabbled, nervously, 'but I can see you're not. Who are you?'

She sat me down before the fire. The other people melted away in the darkness, presumably going to their resting places. I had obviously disturbed them.

The woman stirred the fire with a stick, making it flare and giving us a little more light. I could see that she was quite squat-looking, her chest having sunk into her hips, or so it seemed. Her face was broad and flat, with wide, flared nostrils.

'I'm sure you know who we are,' said the woman,' 'now that you can see me.'

'The *unwanted*,' I replied.

She nodded, vigorously. 'You're safe here, from those above, so you can relax a little.'

I felt the tenseness going out of me. In fact I was exhausted, but there was no way I could just fall asleep. I had to know there and then what was going on. How these *unwanted* came to be still alive.

'I've been down here before,' I told her. 'On the other side. There are lots of skeletons there – of the *unwanted*.'

She nodded. 'That's the old sacrificial area. The Families made a mistake when they changed it to this side of the cliffs. Do you want to hear all this now?'

'Yes,' I cried. 'I *must* hear it now.'

She settled down onto her haunches and began playing with the fire again. The shadows danced over her hammered features. There was a soft look about her that I had not seen in a woman before – some men maybe – but not a woman. Her voice too, was gentle.

'When they changed the place where they threw us over the cliff,' she began, 'they did not realize that below the ledge was a marshy area. It was soft enough for some of us to survive. Of course, the babies died at first – drowned in the mud, or were killed outright by the fall – but one or two of the half-grown children survived and began living in the rainforest. Gradually their numbers increased.

'As they grew to adulthood, they came to realize that there was a way of saving all the *unwanted*, even the babies. They built a net of vines beneath the rockshelf, and caught them before they hit the marsh. That's what you landed in – the net'.

'All this – the netmaking – took place a long while ago. I was one of the first babies to be saved by it.'

I was jubilant. I felt like dancing through the forest and shouting up at the moon. I was alive. I had landed among my own kind. The *unwanted* were fooling their families above. It was good. It was very, very good. I laughed out loud.

'Now tell me your story,' she asked, quietly.

I recounted my recent adventures, slipping back in time occasionally, to speak about my upbringing and the way in which I was treated. The woman grunted encouragingly, every so often, occasionally asking a question. Over the course of the night, she came to learn almost everything about me.

'So, your brother kept you alive. Yet he would not speak to you?'

'It was because he wouldn't speak to me that I'm walking around now. Don't say anything against my brother,' I warned. 'I don't like it.'

She smiled, her face creasing in the grey light of the dawn.

'I think it is good that you are loyal to your brother, but you must realize that to me, he is just another one of them, up there. The butchers that murder their own children. However, we'll say no more about that at the moment. We must learn to know each other first. My name is Turningfast. You called yourself *it* – what did you mean?'

'That's where I went wrong before being born. I'm not a boy or a girl – I'm something in between. I call myself *the shadow*.'

And there we left it for the time being, for after those words I fell asleep.

When I woke the next morning, I found myself by the smouldering ashes of the fire. Turningfast was nowhere to be seen, but there were other people milling around beneath the giant canopy I had seen the night before. The shelter was made of woven palm leaves and served to keep the constant rain from being the nuisance to these people that it had been to Tilana, Clay and me.

I studied the occupants of this village through half-closed eyes, still lying where I had slept. I wanted to look at them, before they knew they were being observed.

There were, it was true, many malformed bodies around the place, though most of them seemed to be making themselves useful at tasks not dissimilar from those the Family carried out of a morning. They were making fishing nets, or spears, or setting off to hunt, or cleaning vegetables. All the chores that need to be done in order to live well.

However, there were also many children and adults who seemed to be perfect in limb and body. This puzzled me for a while, until I saw a child go to its mother. The child was seemingly sound, but the mother was obviously an *unwanted*. Somehow, then, grotesques like myself had managed to have children who were not malformed. But how could that be? All our teachings told us that the *unwanted* were the spawn of evil and surely evil could only begat more monstrous shapes?

Shortly after I was musing over this puzzle, I was brought breakfast by Turningfast.

'How did you get your name?' I asked, between mouthfuls. 'I took mine from my brother. I am his shadow, you see.'

'When I was thrown over the edge of Cloudrock, I was spinning. They called me after that.'

I nodded. 'And so you became Turningfast. That's what I have to call you then.'

She looked a little embarrassed for a moment and I wondered why, until she spoke her next words.

'Not you. You must call me *mother*.'

I looked up, surprised.

'What? Why?'

'You see, when the babies arrive they have to be cared for – and the young children. So they are given parents. I am too old for a baby now, but I asked if you could be given to me. I know you're almost grown, but I would like it if you thought of me as your mother.'

She looked away from me, shyly.

'All right,' I said, scraping my wooden dish. 'I don't mind.'

Her face beamed then.

'And you have many brothers and sisters – children I have raised. Most of them are adults now...'

I held up my hand.

'No. A mother is fine, but I already have a brother and I don't want any more.'

She sighed and shrugged. 'As you wish. We are all Redgod's children.'

'Surely not?' I argued. 'We are not part of the Family. How can we come from Redgod. We are outside the circle.'

Her face flushed.

'Never talk like that here,' she said, in the harshest tones I had heard from her so far. 'We don't believe in *their* teachings of Redgod. We're as good as they are. Although we don't have the same marriage laws, we eat our dead just the same. We have our own circle, just as good as theirs.'

She seemed so annoyed I thought it best to agree with her, though it seemed to me that her argument had too many flaws in it to be acceptable to Redgod. After all, how could you keep the blood pure if intermarriage took place. It didn't make sense.

After I had eaten, she took me around the village and introduced me to a lot of people. There I received the greatest shock of my life. It was such a strange thing that it took my breath away and I could hardly speak. It was this: in the village were people who were not from Cloudrock, or from the rainforest. They came from far away, beyond the Deadlands. Yet they looked just like

107

us – almost. Some of them had red or yellow hair and blue eyes, that was all. I was told that they had set out, on a journey, some time ago. They had wandered in places that were only names to me and had crossed the Deadplace, to find the village of the *unwanted*. That is, they had not known it was there, before beginning their walk, but having found it, they stayed.

I did not want to have anything to do with these people. They talked in a strange way sometimes – even darker than the rocks and trees – and I wondered if they were actually ghouls who were fooling my cousins by taking on the shapes of men and women. I resolved to keep clear of these creatures.

But despite these outsiders, what a calm, peaceful place the village really was. Although there was some bickering among the people, it was nothing so bad as that amongst the Family. They seemed, on the whole, so much more easy with one another. Usually there was good reason for an argument. They didn't snap and snarl at each other the whole time, for no good cause, and the taut nerves that the Family carried around with them all the time, seemed to be absent here.

I was home, at last.

During that first morning I met one of my new 'brothers' – a man called Charcoal (he had a black birthmark under his eye which covered much of his cheek). Despite the fact that he was blind, he managed very well, mending nets and other tasks. I liked him a lot. He had a good sense of humour. He said one thing which made me a little worried however.

'One day, you can show us the way to the top, and we can get our own back on the families of Cloudrock.'

Since my brother was up there, I wanted nothing to do with such a scheme and told him so.

'You might not have a choice,' he replied, his face cocked to one side, listening for my further reply. But I said nothing more. I just slipped away and went out into the forest, to collect my thoughts.

So began my life amongst my own kind. Although we did not live in yurts or caves, we had our own spaces beneath the canopy, which were treated with respect by neighbours. I stayed by my new mother's fire, helping with the chores and bringing in food by fishing or hunting with my catapult. Those above, on

Cloudrock, could not see our fires because we were hidden by the overhang, the forest and the canopy. I knew from my own experience that all that could be seen from above was a vague world of mists and green shadows. I hoped that Clay had found some happiness up there, but I was sure it would be nothing to mine.

Chapter Seventeen

Despite the kindness that was shown to me, I still missed my brother a great deal during those first days amongst the *unwanted*. I took myself off into the forest, to be with the companions of my early years, but for different reasons from those which had first sent me to them.

However, I gradually came to know most of the people in the village, though I steered clear of the outsiders. One youth, called Hagar, seemed particularly taken with me and always called out a cheery greeting followed by a wave. It was a friendliness that was not to last very long.

The language and culture from the top of Cloudrock, in essence, had been adopted by the *unwanted*, though there were some small differences. I suppose older children who had been tossed over the cliff had brought it with them. Anyway, we still had *Good* and *Bad* Days in the calendar, stools for dead ancestors, things like that. Turningfast told me that the next *Good* Day had been put aside for a village meeting, where people could air their grievances, settle disputes and raise any subjects that they felt were worthwhile discussing.

'Are you going?' I asked her.

She ran her fingers through her grey hair.

'Of course. Everyone goes.'

'What about me?'

'You too. You're a member of the community now. It doesn't matter how long you've been amongst us. We're all of equal importance.'

So, as the day approached, I became more excited. The elders were airing their cloaks of parrot feathers and the musicians tightened the skins on their drums and polished their flutes. There was a general feeling of festivity which I had often witnessed on the world above, but had never felt part of. It was all quite overwhelming in those early days. People acknowledged me, spoke to me, shared their fires and their food with me. I was a real person to them, not a shadow.

The morning of the Good Day began with the sound of drums – loud to me there, but hidden by the roaring of the waterfalls to the Families high above. The smoke from our morning fires mingled with the mist as the activity got under way. Turningfast gave me a present of a pigskin loin-cloth decorated with shells. It was the first gift I had ever received and though I was speechless she must have read the gratitude in my expression.

I began the day with a swim in one of the pools and enjoyed myself so much I neglected to watch for logs and was nearly struck by one that came over the edge of the waterfall. Fortunately, Hagar called out a warning and I was able to avoid the missile from above.

Later, we all gathered beneath the canopy in a rough circle and the feasting began. I was surprised to see the outsiders there, but noticed that their women did not partake of a recently dead member of the village. When the flesh was offered to them they shook their heads violently. Such behaviour was a little bizarre, but no one said anything to them.

There was a magnificent dance by one of the hunters, who appeared to be pursued by warrior-ghouls and was displaying his fearlessness of them. He began by letting out a series of savage yells. Then he took his spear and made frantic dashes, back and forth, stabbing at the air. Each charge lasted about twenty paces but was full of menace and threat. The hunter grimaced furiously, each time, and howled and shrieked, baring his teeth with animal-like snarls. During each run he would perform one or two fantastic leaps, high into the air, to display his athleticism to the enemy. All the while, others encouraged him with shrill cries, holding out their hair at arm's length to make themselves appear large and wild.

I became intoxicated by the action, curling back my lips and crouching in ugly poses. I became drugged with frenzied movement, letting the spirit world know that I too would never submit to its warriors.

One of the children was physically sick, with fright.

After this, the talking began and I paid very little attention, until I heard my name.

' . . . the Shadow can lead us to the top. All the young men and

111

women warriors are ready to do battle with the Families. At last we can take our revenge.'

It was Hagar speaking: the young hunter who had been so friendly towards me.

One of the elders asked, 'How do you feel about this, Shadow? Are you prepared to lead Hagar to the passage which joins the two worlds?'

'What for?' I asked.

Hagar said, 'Why, to kill them.'

I shook my head firmly.

'My brother is up there. I think we should leave them alone.'

Hagar's face clouded over with anger.

'Are you with us, or against us?'

All eyes were on me and I felt very vulnerable. I had not prepared for this and I hardly knew what to say.

'I'm not against you. You've all been very kind.'

'Well, then?' said Hagar.

'I won't help in any slaughter. I don't want to.'

Hagar stamped his foot in frustration.

'You must be *made* to.'

Just then there was a stirring amongst the outsiders and a woman elder motioned that they should have their say. A man stood up.

'You all know me,' he said. 'My name is Mecal and I come from . . . across the Deadlands. If I may be permitted to offer an opinion . . . ?'

The woman elder said, 'You are free to speak, Mecal.'

'Well, as a rule I do not like to interfere in village affairs. I am aware that we come from the outside and it is no business of ours how you conduct yourselves, but let me warn you – what you are contemplating here, is *war*. I have seen such wars take place and they are a bloody business. It sounds straightforward enough. You all take your spears and bows and wipe out the enemy. Even if I approved of such killing, which I don't, it's never as simple as that. They will defend themselves. Some of you will die. It is very doubtful that it will all be settled in one go. Some of them are bound to escape and will hide and begin their own attacks on this village. You'll be starting something that has no end.

'At the moment, they don't know we're down here. I suggest you keep it that way. You'll only regret exposing yourselves . . .'

Hagar grunted in disgust.

'All this concern about killing. Why, they've been throwing babies over cliffs since as long as we can remember. It's time we did a little killing . . .'

Emboldened by the intervention of the outsider, Mecal, I jumped to my feet, crying, 'Well I'm not showing you the way. You find it yourself.'

'We will if we have to,' snarled Hagar, 'and I'd be careful if I were you. We have no room for traitors down here. How do we know he's not a spy?' he enquired, attempting to harness the sympathy of the listeners to his cause.

The elder said, 'That's enough wild talk, Hagar. We do not attack our own.' She turned to me. 'Child, are you sure you will not do this thing? We might rid ourselves of the Families for good.'

'No,' I replied. 'I can't. I'm sorry.'

She nodded and sat down, saying, 'You have your answer, Hagar.'

The youth glared at me and stormed off, into the forest. One or two of his friends followed him. I felt uncomfortable, but quite angry myself. Some people were glaring at me, but Turningfast patted my shoulder.

'It will pass over,' she whispered.

I hoped she was right.

Later, during the story-telling which went on well into the evening, an outsider called Mich, told us about a wonderful animal that lived far across the Deadlands. She drew a picture of it in the dust and it had a tail at both ends of its body. She said it was twice the height of the tallest hunter. One of its tails was hollow and it sucked water through this end and blew it out in fountains. I was enthralled by such a beast.

'What colour is it?' I called out.

'Every colour imaginable,' she replied, her eyes sparkling. 'And each colour shines like crystal – brilliant reds, greens, blues.'

'And you've seen one of these creatures?' enquired an elder, just as fascinated with the account as I was myself.

Some of the fizz went out of the story-teller from beyond. She looked round, once or twice, at her group, before replying, 'Well, not exactly. Not a live one. But I have seen rocks carved in their shape and decorated with the colours, as I described.'

'And these carvings were twice the height of a hunter?' said the elder.

'Yes.'

The elder shook his head.

'That does not mean that the real beast was just as large. Perhaps the artist took liberties with size? I can believe in the colours – that seems right – but I would guess that the live animal is much smaller than you think.'

The outsider woman nodded and sat down, muttering, 'Perhaps you're right. I only know what I saw.'

When the day was over, I went to my bed by the fire, and fell instantly asleep. I had bad dreams, full of blood and carnage. I was glad to see the following day, creeping between the leaves of the trees and chasing away the darkness.

Chapter Eighteen

The night after the stranger Mecal had sided with me in my refusal to lead the young warriors to the top of Cloudrock, I went to see him at his fire. He was busy making strange markings on a piece of animal skin in red dye.

'What are those?' I asked.

It seemed to me that he was just making stains, rather than pictures, but he seemed intent on getting them right, according to some idea he had in his mind. He held one up, looking satisfied with it.

'These are called maps, or charts. They help us find the way – or will do, if we ever leave this place.'

For some reason the markings excited me. I felt a wave of energy coming from them that flooded my body and brain with emotion. There were lines that resembled the rings in the trunk of a cut tree and stick-like symbols scattered between them.

'Are they magic?' I asked. 'Like the symbols we carve in our bows?'

He laughed.

'Not really. I wish they were, then we'd never get lost. What they represent is the shape of the land – out there.'

It didn't look like that to me, but then I was not a traveller, like Mecal. Until very recently, I had thought that the whole world was just Cloudrock.

'Does the land always stay the same shape?' I asked.

He looked very thoughtful at this.

'It did, once upon a time – more or less the same shape. Nothing is sure, though.'

'Once upon a time there was water that came right up to the lip of Cloudrock,' I told him. 'That's what the legends say – that the Deadlands were once covered in water – but I don't know whether to believe that or not. It seems impossible – so much water.'

He nodded. 'The legend is true, Shadow. Cloudrock was once a coral atoll – a ring of islands – on top of an underwater mountain.'

'But where did all the water go?'

I had visions of some giant bird, drinking it all up, until the world was dry.

'It moved, somewhere else. We have stories, where I come from, like yours. It looked quite different – all of it – once upon a time. We don't really know what happened but there were earthquakes and floods and volcanic eruptions ...' He explained what some of these things were and I was amazed at the vastness of the landscape beyond our little place. It made me feel very small and frightened inside.

'So the world shook and trembled and pieces of it disappeared, and other pieces built into mountains like this one? Perhaps the earth became angry and rattled itself?' I suggested.

'What?' He seemed amused.

'Well, the earth is live, isn't it? Why shouldn't it get angry, just as we do? That makes sense to me.'

'And who would make it *angry*?'

'Us, of course. If we were doing something which it didn't like? Maybe some of the people at that time threatened the earth with spears and bows and it had to teach them a lesson?'

He cocked an eyebrow at me.

'You're a funny kind of child, Shadow. Where do you get such thoughts from?'

'I don't know – dreams I suppose. Things happen in my head. Don't they in yours?'

'Sometimes, yes, they do. I get peculiar thoughts occasionally, but I try to ignore them. No, I don't think people threatened the earth. Even if it were live, bows and arrows wouldn't frighten it. Disasters just happen sometime, for no reason. I like things with reasons behind them – now take your situation here,' he puffed out his chest and placed the map carefully by his side, 'I've worked out why you have this strange society on Cloudrock.'

'Strange? What's strange about it? It's right, according to Redgod's laws.'

'Ah!' he picked up a stick and waved it in front of my face. 'That's what *you* believe, but I've seen lots of different groups of

116

people and there are not many like you lot. Most people think it's wrong to marry within the family.'

I laughed out loud.

'That's ridiculous. How can it be wrong? It keeps the blood pure.'

His face darkened for a moment and I thought he was going to get angry with me. I prepared my legs to run away, but in the end he spoke calmly enough.

'I don't like that idea of pure blood. It's very dangerous. It makes some people think they are special – better than others. That isn't true. You are as good as your brother. You are as good as me. I am as good as anyone else here. We're all the same.'

'Not the *unwanted*.'

'Yes, even the *unwanted*. Just because your bodies are not perfect for movement – anyway, we're getting side-tracked. Let me tell you *why* your group, your family, are as they are . . .'

Some hunters were returning from the forest – young men and women with their quarry. One or two of them walked a little crookedly, or held their weapons in crippled arms, while others walked straight and tall. They seemed to get on well enough with each other, but perhaps that was because they had to? I didn't really know. It was all getting a little confusing for me.

'You're not listening,' said Mecal, giving my ear a flick.

'Yes I am,' I lied.

'I was saying that perhaps, after the disaster occurred there was a plague of some kind. Tell me, do you eat people that have died of sickness?'

'No. We have to burn them. They are lost to the Family.'

It seemed the right answer, because Mecal was nodding.

'Good. Yes, that fits in. You see, if there was a plague, especially in an isolated place like Cloudrock, from which there was no escape, families would withdraw into themselves. Find a cave somewhere, to hide from those that were sick. The only way one could be sure of getting a mate that was clean, would be to marry within the family.' He seemed to be talking to himself, more than to me. 'Pretty soon, that would become the law, as you call it. You would *have* to marry in the family, to ensure that the disease remained outside your group.'

He stared up at the sky, as if deep in thought.

'The cannibalism – several answers there. Perhaps that came

117

about through shortage of food, at a time when travelling abroad to hunt was dangerous? Or, if a family were in a cave, with nowhere to bury their dead, they ate them to get the bodies out of the way – prevent further disease? It's all very interesting.'

He threw a few sticks onto the fire and we both watched as the sparks flew upwards.

'You see,' he continued, 'things like that don't just come about. They develop through necessity. Now it's no longer necessary to marry your brother or sister, or mother or father, changes are taking place – slowly. I've heard about your brother, Clay is it? And his wife. They are perhaps the first. I wish I could live for a thousand years and watch it all happen.'

I thought about Clay and Tilana. This stranger, Mecal, who seemed to know many strange things – more than all of us put together – thought it was right that they should get married. That was something which was difficult to understand, given that Redgod's laws were inviolable.

Suddenly, Mecal said, 'What was it you wanted, anyway?'

I jerked upright.

'What?'

'You came to see me about something.'

'Oh. I just wanted to thank you for being with me last night, when the young warriors were against me.'

He waved a hand at me.

'Oh, that. Don't give it a thought.'

'Well, I did and I wanted you to know I was grateful. I was afraid of you – you people from the outside – when I first came here. I'm not any longer.'

He stretched out a hand and laid it on my shoulder. I could feel its warmth through my skin. His blue eyes looked into mind.

'That's good. I'm glad. I think we will be good friends, Shadow.'

I was embarrassed by the touch. Until that time very few people, except by accident, had put their skin next to mine. Only my brother, of course, and he was special to me. I wriggled away, when I could, and ran off into the forest to think about things. One aspect of it all was plain to me. I no longer felt that terrible loneliness which had been with me before I came down to live amongst the *unwanted*. It felt good. There was a buzzing inside me as if I were full of warm, furry insects. I had a new mother and a new friend. I had never had a friend before.

However, having made a friend, I also discovered that I had made several enemies too. Not that that was anything new to me. Once upon a time the whole population had been my enemies.

The warriors that were so anxious to go to war with the Families above, did not like me. In fact they hated me because I would not show them the way to the top. They called me traitor and spurned me when the elders were not around to interfere.

Hagar told me: 'Go and hunt with someone else. You're too puny to hunt with us.'

'I don't need to be tall and strong,' I cried. 'I use a catapult, not a spear.'

But they still pushed me aside and became angry if I followed them into the forest. Once, some of the girls were bathing in a pool at the bottom of a waterfall. It was such a peaceful scene, I stopped and sat on the bank to watch them. One of them came and sat by me – a girl named Tallgrass. She lay naked on the bank, drying her brown body in the sun, and talking to me. Then Hagar came along, with some other youths, and started shouting at me, telling me to stay away from Tallgrass. I had no idea why he was so angry, but that evening I put a burr in his bed and watched him spend a restless night.

The following morning he found the burr.

He came to me, by my mother's fire, and accused me of violating his bed.

'I ought to beat you, child. Why don't you go back to where you belong?'

'Ha! You'd like that wouldn't you? So you could follow me and slaughter the Families.'

'You cause nothing but trouble.'

'Me?' I pranced around, looking indignant. 'What about you? I just want to hunt with everyone else, but you won't let me.'

His eyes narrowed.

'As long as I'm around, you'll *never* hunt with us. You're a poisonous little animal.'

With that, he strode away, leaving me feeling sorry for myself. I must admit it hurt me, that he hated me so, but I wasn't going to

119

show it, to him or to anyone else. I just laughed after him, which made him all the more furious and determined never to let me into the group.

The months went by in like manner.

Once, I went out into the Deadlands with Mecal. There was not a great deal out there, except a few rock pools, with crabs, lizards and snakes. It was peaceful though, and dry. Although we had the canopy, the damp air was uncomfortable after a life on Cloudrock. Mould grew everywhere, especially on the animal skins. Outside the camp, if we spent any time there, we had to make an earth oven to cook food. It was not very satisfactory.

The day Mecal and I set out, the sky was flowing over our heads in an effluence of parrot blue and the salt flats came towards us like a white river. Physically, we moved forward, but spiritually, we seemed static. It was almost as if instead of us providing the energy for the movement, it was the world that rolled beneath our feet and we merely lifted our legs in order that we were not swept along with it. The sky rushed over and ahead of us, the earth beneath and against us, with the occasional flights of birds, some in their thousands, flying cross-wise to both of these tidal races.

Out on the flatlands, for we stayed there several days, beneath the cold dog star, I came to know the earth better. I felt its tides, its movements, in my blood. I closed with it, aware of its position in the ebb and flow of the universe. Its paths, its highways, its tracks, were open to my mind. I was the earthchild, the rain-child, the spirit of the landscape. In me were the minerals and rocks, the winds and waters of my birthplace.

There was a day of mist and rain and poor visibility.

Mecal said, 'I think we're lost,' but I knew where I was. Just as I had known, instinctively, which way to go beneath the ground, in the caverns that led from Cloudrock to the rainforest, so I knew here, which way our path lay.

I told Mecal I could sense our path and while he worried and fussed over the maps, he did take note of the direction I said we should take, and we came through the mists to find Cloudrock towering above us.

By noon of the third day there were thin clouds in the sky: dark purple, with bright streaks, like Greatgramma's nose. They raced overhead. I looked back, once or twice, at Cloudrock, stark against the magenta foam that swirled in turmoil about its mushroom shape. It was as if the sky around my birthplace were boiling in dark blood. I mentioned this to Mecal, who shook his head at me, but said nothing.

Mecal said to me once, 'The Families on Cloudrock – what would they think if they saw us out here?'

'They would believe us to be ghosts,' I said.

But his casual remark made me remember my brother and a deep sadness entered my heart. Would I ever see Clay again? It seemed unlikely, unless I were to sneak back to the top and try to catch a glimpse of him while he was out hunting. I tried to put all such thoughts out of my head.

From time to time, we had a new addition to our group. A boy of three arrived in the vine nets one morning. I recognised him as one of the Night Family children, from my time in the cave when the great wind had swept across the island. The child was simple: that was his crime and it was for that reason he had been cast to his death. It made me very angry. Despite my defence of the Families when talking with Mecal, I knew somehow that this sort of thing was not right. To attempt to kill a child, just because its brain did not develop.

Following the boy of three, some two months later, was a baby.

This was an unusual event, because the baby was perfectly sound in limb and body. And it was too young – perhaps two days old – to tell whether its mind was impaired.

'Why would they throw away a perfect child?' I asked Charcoal.

His sightless eyes turned in the direction of my voice.

'I don't know. It is strange.'

'Has it ever happened before?'

'Not to my knowledge.'

Turningfast could not satisfy my curiosity either, so I went to see the baby.

It looked like a normal hunter's child, long in limb and sound in torso. I did not understand it at all. The Family would never throw away a child that might prove to be a powerful hunter – unless – unless there was something unusual about its conception. Obviously, the birth had been successful. It had to be something hidden, something about the actual presence of the child, rather than the physical or mental properties.

Over the next few weeks I watched the baby growing and its features taking shape, emerging from that wrinkled-fruit look that most newly born possess.

When I knew I was right, I went to the elders.

'I want my mother, Turningfast, to have that baby,' I said.

The elders were startled by my request and probably in the assertive way in which it was delivered.

'Turningfast is a grandmother. Leave the child to some of the younger mothers, with babies of their own and milk to give,' murmured an elder.

'Why do you wish the baby to go to Turningfast?' asked another, a little more curious than her contemporaries.

'The baby is my niece – my brother's child,' I said. 'We are close relatives. I want to help in the raising of the girl.'

'Are you sure about this?' asked the same old woman.

'Yes. I can see him in her features. I am lonely down here, without my brother. I want part of him close to me.'

'I can understand that,' she murmured.

They deliberated for a long while, before refusing my request. I was upset, but there was little I could do about it.

'Give me one thing,' I said. 'Just one thing.'

'What's that?'

'Let me name the child. I want to call her – Shade.'

There was a general buzz of conversation and I received reply that, provided the new mother did not object, the baby would be called Shade. I learned later that she was quite willing to give the child that name and I was told that the mother would recognize my relationship. It was something.

You see, I had worked out who the mother really was. It must have been Tilana. This baby was the product of their night of love in the cavern. It was the only reason why the Family would cast her out. She was the product of an unlawful union. They must have been surprised when she turned out not to be a monster, an *unwanted*. I wished I could have seen their faces as they inspected her, probably a hundred times, searching in vain for some defect. I wondered whether the parents knew about the disappearance of the baby, or whether Ruanna, Tilana's brother-husband, had taken it upon himself to rid the new Family of the unwanted child.

Chapter Nineteen

When the fires had burned low one night and the red embers were like hot sores on the ground, I crept from my bed and made my way to the slit in the rock which led to the world above. As I passed by some bushes on the outskirts, I almost ran into a young woman squatting amongst some ferns. Luckily she was too intent on her task to notice me.

I saw what she was doing. Tilana had told me about the practice of virgins breaking their own maidenheads with a smooth stone, so that they were in control of the operation. This is what the young woman had been doing.

I thought about Tilana's jibe: that my father was a glossy lump of granite from the bed of a stream. The idea no longer bothered me. It did not matter that Clay was not my *real* brother. He had not in fact saved me from death: just from a different life. But I found that this made no difference to my feelings for him. He was still the person who had sheltered me from the Family and had therefore *made* himself my brother.

If my father was a pebble, it would explain why I could hear the rocks whispering to one another in their distant, dark voices. It would make me a child of the earth: a child of the rain. I did not mind that thought so much. Born of woman, from stone. Who could ask for better parents? I liked to think that I had been fathered by the landscape. It made me part of it.

I found the opening in the rock and pulled away the dead branches. Then I entered the darkness inside. When I had gone up the last time, my torch had given out halfway to the top. At first I had panicked, but found that it was actually easier in the dark, than when I had been carrying the torch. I had both hands free for climbing and I just allowed my instincts to guide me, feeling my way from handhold to foothold.

It was while I was climbing that I first heard the ominous sounds from the belly of the rock. I paused for a while and

123

listened hard, my ear to the limestone wall. It was not so much that I understood what the earth was saying, but that I absorbed a sense of what it intended. The full force of its threatening tones almost caused me to fall from the ledge, but I clung on and let the emotions pass through me in hot waves. It continued to batter me with its warnings as I climbed out of the pothole and into the cave. Then it stopped.

Once out, onto the top of Cloudrock, I sat on the ground to recover my emotional breath. There was nothing I could do immediately, however, and decided to carry out my original plan. I went down to one of the streams and smeared myself with red mud.

Once I had covered myself with a thick layer, I made my way to my old village. I stopped at the edge of the forest, looking out on the yurts. Everything appeared to be peaceful so I made my way quietly and swiftly to the tent of Yellowbark and slipped beneath the edge.

It was dark inside, but I could hear two people breathing and wondered how I was going to tell which was Yellowbark and which, her brother-husband. I sat there for a long while, by the central hearth wondering and wondering, when eventually one of the sleepers stirred and sat up. By this time my eyes were accustomed to the darkness and I could see the shape of the person against the lighter wall of the tent. I still could not tell which of the pair it was. There was a long period when nothing happened, then a frightened voice said, 'Who's that? Who's there?'

It was Yellowbark.

Concerned in case she woke her brother-husband, I slipped outside and crouched against the ground. After a moment, I heard voices, one of them sleepy and speaking in grumbling tones. Then a man came out and stared around the compound. I crawled quickly beneath the edge of the yurt again.

'Yellowbark, this is the Shadow,' I whispered. 'Back from the dead. If you scream I'll tear out your eyes.'

There was a whimper from the far side of the yurt.

'Meet me on the edge of the forest, or I'll haunt you until . . .' At that moment the tent flap moved and I rolled outside again. I could hear a male voice saying, 'There's no one out there. You're dreaming.'

I ran to the forest and waited. Shortly afterwards a figure came half stumbling, half walking, to the place where the forest path began. By the light of the stars I could see my old enemy and could hear her moaning softly to herself. She must have been terrified.

I stepped out to meet her. I must have looked an awesome sight, with the mud drying and cracking, falling off in flakes. I wondered whether she believed it to be my rotting flesh. She gave a tiny cry and stepped backwards, as if to run away.

'Don't go,' I warned. 'I'll flay the skin from your back with my tongue. I'll boil your heart in your chest with my breath.'

'What do you want?' she croaked.

'I want to burn you to a cinder where you stand, but I have a task to do for Redgod. She's sent me as Her messenger to speak to my brother. You must show me where they now live.'

'It's in the ... in the silk-cotton ... on ...'

'Take me there,' I ordered, 'or so help me, you hag, you'll watch the dawn come up through blistered eyeballs.'

She began walking, keeping her face to the front. I must have been a terrifying sight, my eyes looking out through deep pits of mud. I was enjoying myself.

We followed a path, skirting the lake, and eventually came to the silk-cotton tree. As I drew nearer I could see two tree houses built amongst its branches.

'Go and wake Tilana,' I said, to the still trembling woman. 'No one else. Tell her someone wishes to speak to her down by the lake. Don't tell her who it is. As for you – pray that you never see me again. The next time, I shall come in fire and blood.'

Eagerly then, Yellowbark began to climb a ladder to the lowest branches of the tree and I went to the spot where I was to meet Tilana and washed the mud from my body. I did not want to scare the younger woman with my appearance.

Shortly afterwards, Tilana came walking down the path to the edge of the lake, looking around her. I stood up, so that she could see me and I would not startle her by showing myself suddenly.

'Shadow?' she called. 'Is that you?'

'Yes,' I replied, 'Did Yellowbark tell you it was me? I told her not to.'

Tilana was then quite close to me. She stood in the starlight, tall and straight. She seemed to have grown an inch or two, since the last time I had seen her, and she was more of a woman, less of an adolescent. She seemed confident, unafraid.

'Weren't you scared? When Yellowbark told you I had come back from the dead?'

Tilana stared at me. Although she was unafraid, she was obviously surprised to see me.

'She said you were made of river clay. You look flesh and blood to me.' She reached out and touched my arm. 'It's warm,' she said. 'You're no ghost. You're alive – '

'Weren't you scared though? Of me?'

'I was curious – but I could never be afraid of you, Shadow. You're too gentle. Dead or alive, you wouldn't hurt me. Anyway, I guessed you had tricked her somehow. You were always good at things like that.'

I was a little disappointed. I had wanted to be shrouded in mystery: a figure from the Deadplace.

'How is my brother?' I asked.

Tilana tilted her chin slightly,

'He's well.'

'Does he miss me?'

'It's difficult to tell, isn't it? When he doesn't ever talk about you. But he's not happy. Whether that's because of you, or me, I don't know.'

I had to be satisfied with that. I did not want him to be unhappy, but I certainly hoped that he missed me as much as I did him.

'Why did you come back, Shadow? It's very dangerous for you.'

'I came to tell you that the baby is safe.'

Her large eyes opened even wider. She stared at me for a long time. Then she said, 'Baby?'

'The child that was thrown over the edge of Cloudrock. It was perfectly sound. It must have been yours – and Clay's. It was, wasn't it?'

'She's alive?' The words sounded distant, as if they were coming from a long way off.

'Her name is Shade – my name for her. I'm keeping her safe. I wanted you to know.'

Then her arms reached out, gripped my shoulders in strong fingers. Tilana's eyes were shining, but whether in grief or happiness, I did not know.

126

'My baby is *alive*,' she said, as though she hardly believed it. 'And safe . . .'

'Yes,' I replied, struggling beneath her grasp.

Then she looked miserable for a moment.

'I suppose . . . I can't see her?'

'One day, perhaps. It's too dangerous at the present time.'

She said nothing more, but went and sat down by the lake. The reflections of the stars were floating on the small wavelets raised by the night breeze. I did not know what she was thinking and stood by, uncomfortably, waiting for her to speak to me again.

Finally, she said, 'If there were more babies. Would they live too?'

At first, I did not comprehend what she was trying to tell me. Then the light gradually seeped through into my dull brain. I was shocked.

'You and Clay? You're still . . .'

She turned to face me, defiantly. Her chin was tilted in the way that she had when she knew she was doing wrong but was not prepared to change.

She replied, fiercely, 'Yes.'

'Ruanna – and Clay's cousin-wife . . .'

'They don't know. We're very careful. It was the only way, Shadow. We couldn't go out into the Deadlands. We were too afraid. We would have died out there. But this way – it's not good, but we couldn't think of anything else. And we're still together. The only thing I'm worried about is Clay. He gets so jealous at times – he might one day kill Ruanna.'

'And what about you? How do you feel about *her*?'

'I hate her, but I can see that she's necessary to us. Oh, it's all so mixed up, so confusing.'

She was crying now and I put my arm around her shoulders. There was no real help for them, in this place, but I wanted her to know that I understood. I *think* I understood. It was very difficult for me, but I had seen and experienced so many strange things of late that I was willing to accept the state of affairs amongst them as being the only way they could live.

'I have to go now,' I said.

She wiped away her tears with her hands and looked back at the silk-cotton tree, as if wondering whether to wake Clay. Then she said, 'Where do you live?'

'Down below, in the rainforest, amongst the parrots.'

'Just you and the baby?'

I nodded.

'How did you save her?'

'She got caught in the branches of the palms and fell on a soft bank of moss. I found her and looked after her.'

Tilana gave me a hug, which embarrassed me.

'Thank you, Shadow,' she whispered.

Then: 'Will we see you again?'

'One day.'

With that, she walked back to the silk-cotton and left me standing in the approaching dawn.

I left the lake and began to walk back to the cave to begin the climb down, but something was bothering me. I sensed someone following me after a while. Perhaps Tilana wanted to see where I went, so that she could hold her baby again? I ducked behind a rock and backtracked. Then I saw her.

Standing in the grey light of the morning was a figure I knew well. Yellowbark. She was staring at me, but keeping her distance, as if she were still not sure what it was all about. No doubt she had hidden by the silk-cotton until I had finished talking to Tilana and was now watching to see where I went.

I gave out a screech and she stumbled backwards as if to run away, but then turned and stared again. She was trying to work out whether I was indeed a ghost. The river clay had gone from my body, but that did not mean I was alive and real.

I laughed out loud then and ran towards the sacrificial rock. She followed, trotting on behind.

The sun began to creep above the edge of the Deadlands, sending out its spears of light. I raced towards it, with Yellowbark, hard on my heels. At the edge of Cloudrock, I paused and made an obscene gesture to my pursuer.

'Goodbye, you old hag,' I called. 'I'll be back to haunt you again!'

Then, with my heart pounding, I threw myself over the top.

It seemed to take forever to reach the bottom and I had an awful feeling that maybe I was in the wrong place or perhaps the nets had been taken away, but then I felt myself bouncing on the triple layers of woven vines beneath the covering leaves of the palms. I was safe once again.

I climbed down to the ground and made my way back to the village, hoping that I hadn't been missed during the night.

It was a vain hope. Not only had I been seen leaving the village the night before, but had been followed. Hagar was sitting by my mother's fire, looking smug.

'We know where you've been – and how you got there,' he said, smiling. 'I tracked you to the cave. You've been up there, haven't you? And now we know the path.'

I was devastated.

'What are you going to do?'

He could not keep the triumph out of his voice.

'Do? We're going to destroy them.'

'The elders would never agree.'

He spat on the ground at my feet. His face showed his disdain for the elders and I knew that he had already talked this over with the other hunters.

'The elders can't stop us. And don't think you can warn the Families. I've put a guard on the entrance to the cave.'

'I've already warned them,' I lied.

His face clouded over for a moment and I thought he was going to hit me. But then Turningfast was nearby, having just been for her morning trip to the waterhole. He waved one of his hands in front of my face.

'It doesn't matter. We'll destroy them anyway.'

With that he strode away.

I ran to where Mecal was sitting, on the far side of the canopy. He was busy with his charts again.

'Mecal, the hunters – they're going to war,' I cried.

He nodded. 'So I heard.'

My heart sank at the casual way in which he was reacting to the news. I sat down beside him and studied his face.

'But aren't you going to stop them?'

He did not look up from his work.

'What can we do? We're guests in this village. The hunters have all the authority they need – they have the strength and will of their own kind. I've seen this sort of thing happen before. There's nothing that can stop it, once it gets started. I can't get involved.'

'But you are involved. You're here.'

'I'm only an observer. I can advise, but not order. If the hunters want to go to war there's nothing I can do about it.'

I was appalled.

'Don't keep saying that. Listen – while I was climbing through the rock last night, there were some strange messages coming from the earth. It's going to do something . . . '

He looked up then.

'What?'

'I don't know. I just *feel* that something terrible is going to happen if the people go to war. The earth won't let it happen – not without . . . without . . . '

'What?'

I hung my head. 'I can't tell you exactly. It just sent out warnings that made my hair prickle. Dark words – I've never heard anything like them before. They were loud in my head. Harsh sounds. We've got to stop the young men and women.'

He shook his head.

'Can't do it, Shadow. I'm sorry.'

'You're a fool,' I cried, jumping up. Then I ran away from him, into the forest, to find a place where I could think. I had to find a way to reach the top of Cloudrock and warn my brother and Tilana. If we could not stop the war, perhaps we could avoid it? We could hide somewhere, until it was all over.

Chapter Twenty

Mecal and his people would not get involved, in any way, in the coming war between the *unwanted* and the Family. I tried to tell them that they were part of it all now and that if we did not stop this thing from happening, they might not be able to remain aloof: they would get sucked into it eventually. But Mecal insisted that they were outsiders. It was not their problem, he said.

'Surely, this is everyone's concern? Your opinion is respected here,' I argued. 'Please help me.'

'I'm sorry.' He busied himself with other things as I spoke to him. Trivial tasks that might have waited until the important issues of the day had been settled. I suppose they *were* settled, as far as he was concerned. I felt a great disappointment in him. He had been places, seen things that none of us had experienced. He could have brought that experience to bear on the situation. Used it as a lever to oust Hagar. But nothing I said would make him change his mind. Or any of the other outsiders. They were determined not to 'interfere'. It seemed to me such a pity that their knowledge of the world was wasted on people who kept it tightly contained and did not give others the benefit of its valuable potential.

Thus, Hagar had his way, even with the elders. They finally sanctioned the war, knowing that their young people would not rest now that there was an opportunity to punish those who had cast them out, tossed them into the valley of death.

'You will lead the two most able climbers to the top, through the caves and caverns,' said one of the elders, her head hanging low.

'But I don't want to,' I protested.

'You will lead them and they will mark the way for others to follow.'

'But . . .'

131

'You will lead them.'

I did as I was told. I had no choice. These were my people. They had saved my life and I owed them my services. At least if I went with them, I would be there to watch out for my brother. I had some vague thought, too, that no confrontation would take place: that when faced with one another the two sets of people would see how useless and self-defeating it all was. I certainly had no love for my former people, but my anger was directed more towards individuals, like Yellowbark, whom I considered beneath contempt anyway.

I took the two climbers, a man and a woman, into the labyrinth. This time we took torches to light the way and the path was marked with thread. I was surprised by the bravery of the pair that came with me. Although I knew that they were frightened, they tried not to show it and certainly they kept a tight control on themselves, determined not to allow their fear to deteriorate into panic. Not once did they cry out or show their alarm when confronted by the grotesque rock shapes and dark recesses of the caves. They seemed intent on the task only.

It was a slow business, each of us helping the others over difficult stretches. Eventually we reached the top and we sat and waited for the others to arrive. They came out of the pothole, one by one, their weapons tucked in their belts, or held between their teeth. It was the intention to carry knives in order to cut down spears from the forest, once we reached Cloudrock. This was the next task they set about doing: fashioning the spears and bows.

I was again surprised, but this time by the lack of curiosity they showed in their new surroundings. They looked about them, to be sure, but they did not squeal with delight at what they saw. I wondered why, for I felt it was a far more beautiful place than the rainforest below. I put it down to nervousness: concern over the coming war and its consequences. They cut away, steadily, at the saplings and branches which they would need for their weapons. As I watched them work, Hagar keeping a close eye on me, I wondered about the reaction of the two Families to these creatures. Would they be terrified by their misshapen bodies, their wild eyes, their sometimes crazed expressions? Or would they be amused by the audacity of these unholy, ill-formed *unwanted*, who had escaped death but not the warping of their trunks, the twisting of their souls?

132

I was soon to find out, for we were seen in the forest by a group of hunters from the Night Family. They ran away, no doubt to inform their kin that the woods were full of ghouls and ghost-warriors from below.

Since we had been discovered, there was no need to conceal ourselves longer and we were able to temper the points of spears in fires that we had refrained from lighting while we thought we were hidden. The points were hardened in the flames and the arrows straightened and set.

Turningfast and the older people, with the outsiders, had remained below. So it was with the Families. When we emerged from the woodland, it was the young people of all three Families that awaited us. They stood beyond the tall Wedding Rock, painted and feathered, their weapons in their hands. I searched for Clay and Tilana amongst them, but it was impossible to tell one from the other. They all looked the same: tall, supple hunters, now warriors, decorated with insignia that now formed a disguise.

They shuffled together when they saw us approaching and I knew that they were afraid, not amused or curious. The ghosts of the *unwanted* had arisen from their graves and had come to exact revenge. What a terrifying sight we were too! Looking around me, as we hobbled, shuffled, jumped and ran forward. I was impressed by our formidable appearance. Had the Families been attacked by a horde of giant spiders, they could not have been more alarmed. I am ashamed to say I felt my blood rise to the occasion; the excitement stirring in my veins.

The tall Wedding Rock itself rose out of the ground with near-vertical sides. Continual rains had washed it smooth. There were mosses on the northern side and a single tree that sprouted from a crack halfway up from the base, which was embedded in the hard clay beneath. At midday its shadow was a shrunken dwarf – an *unwanted* – but towards evening it would elongate to become one of the Family. I felt peculiar vibrations coming from the rock and a premonition rippled through my mind. An ominous warning was being signalled, but one which I knew would not be heeded, even if I voiced it to my companions.

The slope on which the rock stood curved gently down towards the lake. Here too, beneath the turf, the rocks were struggling to put forth messages.

'Hagar!' I called.

I wanted to warn him, about the rocks, but he did nothing more than glance momentarily in my direction. He was determined that the battle should take place. This was not a time for words. This was a time for blood, long awaited.

I ran to him.

'Hagar, something's wrong.'

'What?' He seemed distracted, not even looking at me. Suddenly, I realised that he was afraid: terribly afraid. But there was something else there, stronger than the fear. It was, I suppose, a sense of the inevitable. This war *had* to take place. It seemed that everyone there but me knew that, as a fact. Once the opportunity arose, for the *unwanted* to get at their persecutors, then nothing on earth would stop that. They had to avenge themselves and their kind.

'Hagar,' I tried again, 'there's something else here. The earth – Cloudrock – it doesn't like what we're doing . . .'

'Don't be foolish,' he said, but his words were delivered in a kindly tone, almost without admonishment.

'You don't understand.'

'I don't need to understand,' he replied, in a distant voice. 'I *feel*, not understand. This is a thing of the heart, not the head. It must happen.'

'That's just it. We're following the wrong leader. We should be listening to our minds, not . . .'

But he wasn't listening. He began jeering, in a tight strained voice, at the opposition. His cry was taken up by the other *unwanted*, who began waving their weapons and calling insults. Some of them were quite inventive and if the situation had not been so fraught, I might have appreciated them more.

Of course, the other side had to return the catcalls in like kind. Both groups were trying to work up their courage, into a frenzy of hatred. You couldn't just kill someone cold. The blood in your veins had to be simmering and bubbling with anger. You shouted at your opponent, goading a reply out of them, and when the reply did come you became angry at its offensiveness. It was self-generating, but apparently necessary. I could see the faces getting more and more twisted, worked up, as the insults got coarser and penetrated more deeply. Somebody on the other side, incensed no doubt by the sheer audacity of these *unwanted*,

134

in crawling out of their holes to confront *real* people, actually began foaming at the mouth.

Then a silence descended as the two groups ran out of obscenities and oaths. I wanted to find out if my brother and his former wife were there, so I yelled, 'Clay! Tilana!'

Several people turned to stare at me, but they were from my own ranks. I saw no movement amongst the enemy.

Someone threw a spear.

I saw it glisten as it curved gracefully through the air. It hit the turf between the two groups and quivered for a second. All else was still. No one moved.

There was a small cry from our ranks. A young man stumbled back two paces and then turned and fled towards the direction of the cave from which we had emerged. In the silence I could hear him gasping for breath and sobbing, and my heart went out to him in his fear. I wished they all had the sense to do what he was doing. I wished they all had the courage to be cowards.

'Go home!' I shouted. 'All of you.'

Some stared at me stupidly, as if I were insane. Others seemed to be angry, and muttered amongst themselves. A great many became nervous, however, and slapped at flies with quick, jerky movements, wondering, I supposed, what they were doing there, waiting to have their bowels torn out by some cruel hook.

The heat of the day was pressing down on the warriors. They were all used to the sweat of toil, but not of idleness. There was a black cloud of attendant flies buzzing over the two groups, like a vapour of dark thoughts made manifest.

Then suddenly, as if by a signal, one person from each side darted forward. Which had triggered the action of which, I do not know, because I failed to see who started first, but these two ran out to meet one another in single combat.

The man from our side was Hagar. I strained my eyes, trying to see who was the warrior from the Family. I was relieved to see that it was a woman and therefore could not have been my brother, Clay, attempting to prove himself after his disgrace. Hagar and his opponent could have been two lovers, rushing to embrace one another after a long absence. It was a chilling sight.

Hagar drew back his arm. I could see the wiry muscles of his shoulder driving the javelin forwards. A momentary darkness came upon me and something deep within me reached out to the

135

other runner. I knew then who it was. Tilana. She was the one attempting to prove her worth before her kin.

The spear was launched.

Suddenly, there was a note in the air that grew in volume to a shriek which made me clap my hands over my ears. It grew louder. The noise changed in pitch, several times, until there was a terrible grating scream and pieces of shale began to shower down from the top and side of the great Wedding Rock.

The ground shuddered beneath our feet and from the forest, hundreds of birds were taking flight. Creatures of all kinds were darting from its recesses, zig-zagging in terror as the earth trembled. Cracks began to appear down the tower of rock. Men and women fell and were burying their heads in their hands. The monolith was splitting into two halves.

One side of it fell into the forest, bringing down trees and crushing bushes. People were thrown into the air as it struck the earth, and other trees vibrated, sending out a humming note which hurt the ears. Sods of earth showered the area.

The other half, the largest piece, came down like a mountain. The falling shadow passed over me quickly, like a cold ghost, as the megalith dropped through the sunlight. This time, the whole of Cloudrock shook on its stalk. A boom went out, over the landscape, in a clap of ground thunder. We were all shaken up, as easily as seeds in a gourd.

When I had regained my feet, Hagar was nowhere to be seen. I ran to the fallen rock, realizing that he had been standing directly underneath it. All that remained of him was a few braids of hair which appeared to be growing from the line where stone met earth.

On the far side, I could see that his spear, flung just before the rock came down, had found its mark. A tall, lean hunter was bent over the prone form of Tilana. The javelin was wrenched from her breast, but she lay as still as death. I could not see whether the person who now lay across her body was Ruanna or Clay.

It hardly made any difference.

I had no doubt that the stone was a warning that we were rousing the earth to anger again. This time I found sympathetic listeners. Both groups had been so badly frightened by the incident, the war was forgotten for that day. We made our way disconsolately back to the exit to Cloudrock, leaving the Families to take care of Tilana. The youth draped over her body had indeed been Clay and it distressed me to see just how grief-stricken he was. I felt sure that one day he would want to know his own child, Shade, for she was part of Tilana and only in the child would he recapture his Tilana. Since she was his daughter, I saw no problems with a possible future marriage. After all, he would only be in his late thirties, when she became of marriageable age. And she was not, truly, an *unwanted*.

Chapter Twenty-one

Somehow, we lost two people in the tunnels. I don't know how it happened – I was up at the front – but they must have taken the wrong turning and disappeared into the maze of caverns and drops along false passages. By the time we reached the village in the rainforest, we were in a sorry state and everyone immediately went into mourning for the three dead souls. No one now needed convincing that the whole affair was a stupid show of pride.

I went to remonstrate with Mecal. I didn't see why he should not shoulder some of the blame for the loss of life. He was not contrite. He played with the twigs he was throwing on the fire and said, 'It was not for us to interfere.'

'Yes it was,' I argued. 'You should have helped me. Anyway, Hagar, Tilana and two others are now dead. Perhaps that will convince people.'

I also told Mecal about my plan for marrying Shade to my brother and was surprised at his reaction.

'Now that *is* wrong. The poor child should be given the choice of a husband and I certainly don't approve of this practice of marrying one's near kin.'

He spoke with such heat he made me doubt the wisdom of my idea.

'But that's how we do things,' I said, defensively.

'What you don't realize,' he replied, still angry, 'is that this is what causes some of your people to be born crippled in mind and body. It's not up to me to tell you how to live, but I want you to know that I totally disagree with this business.'

I went away from him feeling that *I* was the one in the wrong, and somehow I felt cheated. How did he know where the *unwanted* came from? Did he have some magic spying-hole into the mind of Redgod? If it had been anyone else that had said it, I would have laughed it off as ridiculous, but Mecal always spoke with such conviction. He never said anything unless he believed in it, totally. I mean, the business of the war. I might not have liked the fact that he dissociated himself from our affairs, but I respected his firmness.

So, for Mecal and his kind, marrying within the Family was wrong! That was a new twist to life that had me very puzzled. I would have to think about it some more. Anyway, it was all academic. I had forgotten that Clay was married.

Two days later, we woke to find that Mecal and the outsiders had gone. They had packed most of their belongings and set off, presumably, over the Deadlands. They had told no one they were leaving and I was most disappointed in him. He might have said *something*. Then I found the gift by my bed. He had left me a present – a looking-glass that I had always admired. I immediately forgave him.

We had other things to think about, besides fickle outsiders. Over the last two days the air had become foul. There was something in it which hurt our throats when we breathed, and made our eyes water. It stung the inside of our noses and left our lids sore. Above Cloudrock, was a tall bank of vapour.

I had smelt mist like that once before and remembered where: from the crack in earth that separated the rainforest from the Deadlands. What it all meant, no one knew.

The day after Mecal had left, I was out hunting with my catapult in the forest. I was following a spoor left by a wild pig, which had gone up the slope, towards the underlip of Cloudrock. As I followed the tracks, I heard a shrill whistle and my heart stopped. I knew that sound! After only a moment's hesitation, I ran in the direction of the whistle and came to a clearing, in the middle of which sat my brother, Clay.

I let out a whoop, and immediately regretted it, for he looked quite startled. His head turned away from my direction and I knew then that everything was all right. My brother had missed me. He had come looking for me at last.

Poor Clay. He looked a shadow of his former self, thin and wasted, and was no doubt still mourning the death of Tilana. I had never understood this love of his, but it was obviously something that went very deep. Perhaps I was not meant to understand. Anyway, he had not acknowledged me, so everything was still all right between us, despite all that had passed.

I went up to him and hugged him.

He climbed to his feet, somewhat wearily, as if his bones ached as well as his soul, and looked about him. I realized then that he wanted me to take him somewhere and the only place that could be was the village of the *unwanted*.

My concern was, of course, what they would do to him. I was not about to deliver him up to his death, whatever he wanted for himself. I led him back to the edge of the village and hid him in some bushes. Then I went to the elders.

'My brother has come down from Cloudrock. I think he's here as a messenger.'

Drystick, the most senior of the elders raised her bushy, white eyebrows.

'You think? Hasn't he got a tongue in his head?'

She had forgotten what had only recently been told to her. Drystick was at that age when she could remember her childhood vividly, but could not remember with any accuracy the events of the previous day.

'My brother doesn't speak to me,' I told her again. 'He does not see me. All he sees is a shadow.'

Twicemuddy nodded his head. 'I think I remember the girl telling us . . .'

'I'm not a girl,' I said, becoming a little exasperated by their density. 'If I ask my brother to come into the village, can you guarantee his safety? I won't let him be found, if the others are going to hurt him.'

The three elders nodded to each other.

'Tell the boy to come forward,' said Twicemuddy.

'What about the others?' I insisted.

Drystick sent for one of the young girls, who was then asked to run through the village, proclaiming that a visitor had arrived from Cloudrock, who was not to be assaulted in any way.

I went and fetched Çlay. By the time I brought him back, there was a huge crowd in front of the log on which the elders sat.

Clay went before them, his head held high. He looked very dignified and I was proud of him.

'Speak, boy,' said Whitewater, the youngest of the elders. Her hair was only just turning grey and if you wanted anything done quickly, you went to Whitewater first.

Clay said, 'I come as a representative of both of the Families,

the Night and the Day. Since you attacked us a short while ago
. . .' There were murmurs amongst the *unwanted*. I don't think
they liked the implication that we were the aggressors, even
though it was true. '. . . since that time, the air has been almost
unbearable up there. The hole left by the falling of the Wedding
Rock is breathing out bad gas. Some of my people are already
sick – especially the children and the elderly. Soon, we shall all be
unable to fill our lungs with clean air, if we do not find a place
where the gases cannot reach.'

Drystick said kindly, 'What is it you want?'

Clay seemed to give a heavy sigh, as if he had some unpleasant
news to impart.

'Will you let us come down here, until the air clears? We shan't
make any trouble and we'll find our own food and drink. We'll
bring our shelters with us – our yurts – and camp on the far side
of the ridge. We're too weak to fight you. We just want to save
the lives of the children.'

'What about our children – you didn't worry about us, did
you?' cried a voice from the crowd. 'Throw them over Cloudrock,
the way you did us.'

Clay went very red and stared around him at the many
misshapen bodies and grim faces. Whether he had flushed
through anger, because these ugly *unwanted* were taunting him,
or whether he indeed felt shame, I never found out. I believe it
was the former: that he considered these people of whom he had
come to ask a favour, as beneath him, and was only managing to
refrain from spitting out an insult by remarkable self-control.
Luckily for him, however, the kindly Drystick thought he was
contrite and she said, 'Leave the youth alone. He has a distasteful errand to perform. We can at least show our superiority to
those above, by treating him with respect, though I don't doubt
there are few among them who deserve it.'

She turned to Clay.

'Boy, the air down here is very bad too – can't you feel it? Can't
you smell it?'

'Compared with ours, it's as pure as a new morning,' replied
Clay.

Whitewater said, 'I think we should let them come down. The
youth is right. No one can fight in air like this. We can't let them
all suffocate – as yet, the children are innocent.'

Twicemuddy disagreed.

'It's probably some sort of trick. Once they get down here, they'll cut our throats while we sleep.'

'We can keep watch,' said Whitewater. 'We'll have the same advantage as them.'

'That's right,' replied Clay, 'we can watch each other.'

There was a hawking and spitting from Drystick, as she cleared her throat of phlegm. Some of the discarded saliva landed near to Clay's foot. To give him credit, he did not even flinch, though it must have been distasteful to him in the extreme.

Drystick then went into a fit of coughing before saying, 'I agree with Whitewater. Look at the boy. He's as thin as a sapling. Have you eaten recently?'

'No one can eat in that air up there. It just comes back up again. There was one called Tilana,' his voice did not falter, 'who died in the battle. She was the last meat to be eaten – by the women, of course, but the men are no better in holding down their food. The situation is very bad . . .'

'Let them come, let them come,' some of the *unwanted* began murmuring. I think they were impressed by my brother. I know I was.

In the end, Twicemuddy gave his consent, along with the other two elders.

'. . . but,' he said, with a smile, 'we were serious about throwing the babies and children over the edge of Cloudrock. It might be the easiest way to get them down. The adults too. There are nets underneath, to catch them, which is why most of us *unwanted* are here today. There might be a few injuries, but probably far less than if you all tried to come through the tunnels.

'Show him the nets. He won't believe what we tell him. He'll think we're trying to get rid of the Families all in one go.'

Laughing, a group of shambling *unwanted*, crooked of limb but full of heart, led him, tugged him, along the path to the edge of the overhang, where they showed him the nets. Some of the youngsters climbed trees and jumped down into the nets, to show him the spring and bounce of the vines. He smiled – ironically, I think, but they thought he was showing his admiration – and walked away.

Before he left, to fetch his people from Cloudrock, I thrust something into his arms for a moment. It was Shade. He looked down at her face with a lack of comprehension, wondering, I supposed, why this child had been pushed into his hands. Then, gradually, as he stared into the infant's eyes a change came over him. I could see he recognized the child – or perhaps the features of his lost Tilana – because he stared at her so intently. Then suddenly Shade smiled up at him and the expression was contagious, creeping to his own eyes and mouth. The 'mother', who had been holding the infant earlier, reached out her arms now. I suppose she was afraid that Clay would keep her, but he handed her back gingerly and without comment. I felt sure that contact had been made between father and child and it made me feel very good.

Then Clay turned and ran. It was the run of old: full of supple vigour. Once again he was as lithe as a cat and the hunter's heart beat within him.

Some came down the quick way, into the nets: mostly children and young adults. They looked terrified. It might have been the actual jump that had frightened them, but it was probably a nasty experience for them, on landing, to find themselves surrounded by groups of *unwanted*, with their distorted features and misshapen bodies. A wobbly people. Not all of them, of course, but enough to frighten a youngster already feeling insecure.

There were one or two broken limbs from the falls, but nothing terribly serious.

The others all came down through the tunnels and again there were a couple of casualties, mostly amongst the very old, who no doubt had to be virtually carried and lowered on ropes down narrow chimneys and passages. They were a physically strong people though, if nothing else, and there was no lack of courage amongst them. They too, looked badly shaken, when confronted by us, and remained in tight groups as we herded them to a place which was suitable for a camp. One which could be watched by us from a distance, so that we might get warning if they were not sincere about the truce.

We understood that some had remained behind, on Cloud-rock, refusing to leave. Preferring instead to brave the choking air. To certain of them, death was the lesser of two evils.

143

It was this group that tossed down the poles and skins of the yurts, to be caught by the nets of vines. Once these were in the hands of the Day People, they seemed to gain a little in confidence. Perhaps it was having work to do that took their minds off their predicament? But the Night Hunters were a sorry crowd, their large eyes streaming and their lungs wracked with coughing fits. Not that they were the only ones who were suffering: we all were.

Once the initial excitement was over, we continued with our recently developed pastime, of trying to find pockets and areas of the forest where the bad air had not reached, but it was an almost hopeless task. Wherever we went, it seemed to creep after us, to attack our eyes, noses and mouths. Pretty soon we would have to go out onto the salt flats of the Deadlands to escape it.

Chapter Twenty-two

For the next few days the world was full of chanting and singing, as everyone pleaded with Redgod to purify the atmosphere. I made sure that everyone knew about the warnings from the rocks. This bad air was a punishment, I told them, for starting a war among ourselves. If we promised Redgod and the earth that no more fighting would take place, we stood a chance of being forgiven.

Some took notice of me, but others preferred to remain with more traditional chants, requesting clear, bright mornings and the return of the sun, now obscured from our vision.

I went to see Clay as often as I could, which made some of my people suspicious. There were those among the Families who viewed my comings and goings with distrust too. One of them was that old hag, Yellowbark. She watched me through narrowed eyes, saying nothing but showing much in her expression.

Another person I saw occasionally, was that wizened old crone, Nithma, the Greatgramma of the Night People. Her tongue was not still, however.

'So,' she said, 'the shadow has put on flesh. And grand flesh it appears to be.' She spoiled the comment with a snort of derision at the end and I realised she was being sarcastic.

She still looked as if a puff of wind would blow her away, leaning on her stick, her woody face with its bright eyes following my movements as I tried to hurry past her. She scared me more than anyone else I knew.

'Go on, go on. Run away,' she cackled.

'I'm just going to see Clay,' I muttered.

'Thought I'd be dead, didn't you?' she crowed. 'I'll outlive you, you hunchy-back. There's nothing left of me but a husk, but I'll still be here when you're on your last breath.'

'I don't care,' I replied, wanting to be out of her sight.

She smiled that red-crescent, toothless grin of hers and nodded her head.

'Yes you do. Yes you do.'

When I was far enough away, I turned and in cowardly fashion, yelled back at her, 'They won't eat you when you die! That dried-up carcass will stick in their throats and they'll spit you out again.'

She laughed at that.

'I'd like that, then I could plague you forever, because they'll *never* eat you. We'll be going to the same place, dwarf – the land of ghouls.'

Wicked old woman. I hoped she would be turned into a slug and spend eternity trailing around in snot.

The air grew steadily worse, until we realized that we would have to go out, onto the Deadlands. This frightened everyone except me. Having already been out there, with Mecal, I knew there was nothing to be afraid of, but to the others it was a place full of strange monsters and lost souls.

Nevertheless, we had to go. People were becoming very sick. We made sledges to carry provisions and those too infirm to walk, using vines as halters. A rough bridge was constructed over the chasm below, which was now belching out huge clouds of the stinging gas, as if the earth were gasping for breath.

We joined forces with the Families and mobilized. There was little point in going out onto the wastes in separate groups: we had to help each other. All hands were necessary in order to transport the sick and the elderly.

Strange friendships formed in those days of preparation, between *unwanted* and Family people. It was the children that brought them together. The innocent young played with each other as if there were no difference between them. Of course, even amongst the children there were taunts and jibes, but each gave as good as they got, there being no feeling of inferiority amongst the *unwanted*. Like most children, they played, they fought amongst themselves when things went wrong and they made up afterwards, with no grudges borne.

The adults, on going to fetch their youngsters of an evening, would pause to exchange a few words, gradually getting to know one another. There were many who would not have spoken to one from the 'opposite' side if you tortured them with red-hot sticks, but *some* did, and found that they were not so very different from each other, on the inside.

So we went out, the Families with their yurts, and us with makeshift lean-to shelters. We took with us pigskin bags of water and unripe coconuts for drink. We dried the meat of birds and animals and took basket loads of sunbleached fruit. Out on the flats, we found snakes and lizards and other kinds of creatures. All these went into the pot. We had never been too fussy about our diet anyway.

At first we camped as close as we could to Cloudrock. I suppose we were unwilling to break the umbilical cord in those early days. However, the gas followed us, forcing us further and further away from the place of our birth.

Nights out on the Deadlands were unpleasant at first. Most of the adults were terrified and the children cried almost all night long. Since birth we had had it instilled in us that this was the land of rawhead and bugaboo. Here the ghosts of the *unwanted* roamed and it did not make it any more comforting for my people that it was the lost souls of their own dead that roamed the wastes. You can be just as scared of the spirits of your own kind as you are of the phantoms of another group. Ghosts are not particular about who they haunt, and rawheads will rip open the bowels of a brother and sister just as willingly as they will a stranger's.

People talked about the stink of evil in the air, but all I could smell was the foul breath of the earth, drifting out from the homeland. It gathered in billows, that rolled over the flats, engulfing our camps and pushing us out into the undulating lands beyond reach of our beloved rainforest.

The day came when the elders confronted me.

'Shadow, you talked a great deal with the outsider, Mecal, when he was with us. You must have learned the secrets of his travels. How he moved from place to place, yet still knew where he was.'

I replied, 'He carried with him *charts*, which helped him find the way. We have no such magic drawings.'

Drystick said, 'But we understand that when you were out here, with Mecal, you lost your way and it was *you* who led Mecal back to the rainforest.'

I nodded. 'That's true, but I did it by instinct. I *feel* my way, using the messages from the rocks, and the tones of the earth. You wouldn't understand.'

'We don't need to understand,' said Whitewater, 'we need someone to lead us to the far side of the Deadplace. We can't stay here and we can't go back – not until the air over Cloudrock has cleared. Soon we will run out of food and water. Someone must lead us across the wastes, to the places of which Mecal and his people spoke. We have to find an area where there is water and vegetation.'

Me. They wanted *me* to lead them? But I was just the Shadow. A mere black, flimsy whisp of a thing, that followed, not led. Yet I felt my spirit rise within me. I knew that this was right: that I was indeed the one who should take on this role.

'What about the Families? They would never accept such a thing – one of their *unwanted* being appointed over them?'

Twicemuddy had an answer.

'We propose to put to them a joint leadership plan – you and your brother, Clay. In fact, Clay would be merely a figurehead. You would be the one to make the decisions.'

I shook my head in puzzlement.

'I still don't understand why you have so much faith in me. Why me? Why not one of the others?'

'Mecal came to us before he left,' said Drystick. 'He told us that if ever we had to leave Cloudrock and the rainforest, we should trust in your sense of direction to take us across the wastes.'

'But why didn't he take us himself? Didn't he want the responsibility?' I felt that the outsider had let us down.

'He said that we had to make our own destiny, whatever that means.'

So that was how I became the leader of the great caravan, that set forth towards the hazy, distant horizons of unknown lands. Nithma came to see me, before we set out.

'Grander and grander,' she said. 'Such a day I thought I would never see, when a boy and his shadow did what should be the duties of people like myself.'

I was still nervous of her.

'We're not trying to usurp your position,' I said. 'We're just what Mecal called "navigators". You still sit in judgement over

148

Family quarrels and you are responsible for seeing the laws are upheld.'

'Hhumph. I'm not convinced.'

'Well I'm sorry for that.'

'So am I,' she said. 'You have your enemies too, Shadow. I'm not one – you can be thankful for that. I have the intelligence to see that we need you. But Yellowbark – now *she* would rather see you dead.'

'I can handle Yellowbark,' I replied, huffily.

'I hope you can. Anyway, I'll do what I can to keep her from interfering.'

'Thankyou, Nithma.'

'Greatgramma, to you,' she snapped, and hobbled away to her yurt, muttering to herself under her breath. What an old witch she was, but one with enough brains to put her emotions to one side and follow her head. I respected her a great deal.

Chapter Twenty-three

What a wailing went up, when they learned that we were not to go back, but forward, into the unknown. There were those who lay on the ground, kicking and screaming. There were those who wandered around in a daze, looking hollow and abandoned. There were the defiant ones, who sat on one spot and announced that nothing would move them. There were those who actually turned round, and retraced our steps, only to be beaten back, coughing and spluttering, by the cloud that dogged our tracks.

Eventually, the elders and Family matrons restored enough calm for us to move ahead.

Clay and I took the lead, moving way out front, to show the people that there was nothing to fear. Many longing looks were cast back, at Cloudrock, and not a few of those from Clay and myself.

There was still no recognition of me in Clay's eyes. There did not need to be. This was the way it began, this was the way it would end, and this was the way we preferred it. We had returned to our companionship of old, when we would go out hunting together. Except for one difference. Clay followed my lead.

I felt strong. The blood rushed through my veins, exhilarated, effervescent. I knew my path and my brother was at my side. I would never know the love between a man and a woman, but I knew a companionship that was not fraught with the anxiety and fears of sexual love.

I felt strong. The stars suddenly formed patterns for me, each a signpost to a different track. I felt the magnetism of the earth in my bones: the pull of its tides and the sway of its dust. I knew its directions, its turns, its dimensions. All its colours were revealed to me. All its secrets opened like flowers for my inspection. I was part of its rocky depths, its airy high regions. I had found myself in it. I knew what I was and where I was bound.

Clay had confidence in me, that much I knew too. At the end of each day, when we rejoined the groups, he spoke enthusiastically of the progress we had made and the things which were to come: the lands flowing with clear springs and deep rivers. We were a plain, simple people, and would be satisfied with these.

Now that we were well away from the pursuing gas, the livestock began to recover and started to breed again. There was sparse grazing out there on the flats, but the animals soon adapted to the change of diet. Those that did not, died, and we ate them.

One evening, as I was sitting contemplating the rush of scarlet in the sky and the souls of my ancestors gathering for a last social discourse, before the dark settled on the land, Clay came by.

I had hung the looking-glass left me by Mecal on a post – a staff stuck in the ground – close by me. Clay paused by this, staring into the reflection. He had seen his own image before, of course, in the waters of the lake and in polished metal, so I knew that what was fascinating him was not the sight of his own face.

I glanced up at him, wondering why he was so taken with the object, and caught him staring at me via the glass, a bewildered expression on his face.

He stood there, studying me, for quite some time. There was no alarm evident in his features. Just a kind of wondering, which had brought a small frown to his brow. Then suddenly, he gave out a deep sigh, and left me, abruptly. Whatever he had seen in that glass, it had clearly not answered all his questions and had perhaps opened up the ends of a few more.

One thing pleased me. I noticed that he visited his daughter often. The mother had got over her initial jealousy and even welcomed his attentions towards the child. He played with her and taught her all those things a father should. He became an adult.

I saw very little of his cousin-wife, Fantail, who was a shy girl who preferred the company of her mother to that of other members of her Family, or us *unwanted*. To tell the truth, Clay didn't seem to have much to do with her and I rarely saw them in each other's company.

Chapter Twenty-four

Several days passed. We forged salt streams and crossed lakes. The going was hard and our bodies became exhausted through constant work and lack of good food. Much of our diet consisted of landcrabs and lizards, and the occasional bird. Hollows appeared on bodies, which fatty tissue once filled. There were distended bellies and dark rings around eyes. Fever was a constant companion.

Then one clear morning we woke to find ourselves on a ridge. There was excitement in the camp and people were pointing back, in the direction of Cloudrock. I turned my eyes in the direction of the pointing arms and saw what some had already seen. Far in the distance Cloudrock was visible. It was sparkling in the morning sunlight. It looked clean and bright. The cloud of gas had gone.

Immediately, there was talk of returning. A great crowd gathered around the elders and Greatgrandmothers and the most vociferous in her demands that we all about turn and retrace our steps, was Yellowbark.

Her wild hair waved in the breezes as she cried, 'I told you we should have waited a little longer. All this suffering for nothing! I say we go back *now*. Why wait any longer.'

I stood in opposition to her. I sensed something wrong with the situation. There was a dark patch somewhere, which, though I could not put it into words, troubled me a great deal.

'I think we should hold on for a few days, just to make sure that it's going to stay clear,' I said.

Yellowbark sneered, her hands on her hips. Her face was tight with the smile of triumph. A light had come to her eyes, which I knew of old.

'Oh, yes. The Shadow would like to wait. Why not? If we went back now, it would rob him of his newly acquired status, wouldn't it? Look at him. He likes being the leader of all these people. He revels in it. Power! He thought he had us all just where he wanted us. How do we know he's not leading us all to our deaths? Don't you see,' she cried, turning to her own people, her belly thrust out in defiance, 'this is his revenge for so-called ill-treatment as a child. Well, we don't need these *unwanted* now. Let *them* go on.'

There was a silence, during which people just looked at one another. Then they began to separate into their two distinct groups: the Families climbing to their feet and standing aside from the *unwanted*. She was ruining it all. People had just begun to forget their differences, had begun to melt into an homogeneous group.

Then something wonderful happened.

Clay got to his feet and stood there. He seemed to be uncertain about something and for a few moments looked around him at the *unwanted*. He was the last of the Family remaining amongst the people of the rainforest and I could see the impatience scoring Yellowbark's face, as she waited for him to join her.

Then he stepped very determinedly out of the *unwanted* and stood by my side, his arms folded. He said nothing, but his allegiance was obvious. He had faith in me. He valued my judgement.

Yellowbark's expression changed from one of disbelief, to anger.

'Of course,' she said shrilly, 'we expect to find one or two traitors amongst us. The renegade son! The murderer. The matricide. Why not? What else could we expect of a law-breaker, who steals a brother's wife and lives with her in sin? Let them rot out here together.'

There were murmurs of assent from the Families.

'I wouldn't be surprised,' continued Yellowbark, unable to let it rest, 'if some brave soul did not slit their throats before we left.'

Drystick cried, 'Enough of this talk. It's one thing to discuss turning back. Quite another to incite murder and mayhem.'

'You be careful you don't join them,' snapped Yellowbark.

But she had overreached herself with this remark. Drystick was a respected elder of the *unwanted* and the people of the rainforest had not forgotten old wounds and the injustices of the past. They rose, almost as a body.

The two groups began to square up against one another.

153

I said, 'Look, remember what happened last time we did this. People were killed and we all regretted it. If we must split into two camps, then let's do so without any violence. If the Families have decided to go home, that's up to them, but we are going on.'

Whitewater then turned to me.

'Shadow, you must not assume because we take your side in this that we agree with you about not returning to Cloudrock. It is obvious to all of us that we must turn back. We must go to what we can see, rather than on into the unknown. I thought you realized that.'

'But it's a mistake,' I argued. 'I *feel* it. You must trust me.'

'Your heart is in the right place, Shadow,' said Twicemuddy, 'but Whitewater is right. The way lies in the direction of Cloudrock.'

At least, this dissention between me and the elders defused the situation a little and the two groups were able to move apart, without any blood being shed. I could see that only Clay and myself were for going on – perhaps not even Clay, for he hadn't said so – and there was nothing I could do which would change their minds.

During that day, I watched the two separate peoples gathering together their belongings for an early start the next morning. They were excited, chattering amongst themselves and talking of Cloudrock and the rainforest. If they had not been so disparate and I had not this smear, this blemish that darkened my mind, I would have been happy for them. But the rocks were giving out ominous warnings and I knew I had to heed them. I would not be going back.

Clay stayed by my side for the rest of the day. We were like two souls cast adrift from the others. We wandered about looking lost and once or twice I caught Yellowbark, smirking in our direction. That smile of triumph! It was like a spear driven into my heart. I would have given anything to have seen it wiped from her mouth, but she had won. I had to accept that. There was nothing for me to do but suffer her moment of glory. Failure is a terrible beast. It devours you with one swallow, and you feel you will never be the same person again.

It was a fragile evening.

The air was tranquil and there was a fragrance on the light

154

breeze blowing in the direction of Cloudrock. There was a delicacy to the landscape which disturbed, rather than filled me with well-being. I could sense a vulnerability to the scenery. Soft shadows flowed over retreating sunlight: shadows of clouds, like a dark, silent flood. The light from the evening star was hard and sharp: a wounding light.

I turned at a sudden sound behind me. Yellowbark was there. She had followed me. There was a knife in her hand.

'What's this?' I said.

Yellowbark smiled.

'It's something I should have done when you had no power – when you were nothing. I may not get another opportunity.'

I backed away a couple of paces.

She said, 'There's nowhere to run to, Shadow.'

'The others will hear,' I said. 'You'll . . .'

She stepped forward and hit me in the side with the knife. It was an awkward movement, because I twisted away from the blow. There was a numb sensation just above my hip and I gasped in fright. Yellowbark was breathing quickly as she moved in for a second strike.

I reached forward and grabbed her wrist, but she was a powerful woman and I couldn't wrest the weapon from her grasp.

'It's no good,' she wheezed, 'you're going to die. I'll take the consequences later.'

'Why?' I wanted to know.

'All this,' she said. 'This is your fault. Your's and Clay's. Everything started to go wrong when you two broke the laws. Of course we're being punished – but when Redgod sees what I've done to you . . . I promised her you see. That's why the bad air has gone from Cloudrock.'

While she spoke, we wrestled for possession of the knife. I could feel the blood seeping out of my wound. There was no pain, but the shock to my system had weakened me. She was winning.

Then she broke away from me. I turned to run, expecting at any second to feel the blade sink between my shoulders. Glancing behind me I saw that she hadn't moved. Her eyes were on the horizon, looking towards Cloudrock.

Suddenly, a ripple ran over the surface of the ground – a

tremor that set the rocks quivering in the ground and loose stones rattling all around us. Yellowbark fell to her knees. The small hills around us began to thrum and shake in earnest, and a distant rumble built in the throat of the earth: a growl that gradually rose in pitch, until it was a shrill whistle – the sound of a giant in pain.

Then came the explosion.

It came from far off, a thunderous roar that rushed over the Deadlands and reverberated, loosening its roots. I was flung backwards and fell, heavily. The earth gave a tremendous heave, as though it were rolling over in pain. Then the sky lit up: a brilliant red.

I scrambled to my feet as the distant roaring continued and the sky inhaled fire from the ground. Streaks of scarlet flashed over my head to disappear beyond the shoulder of the earth. Tongues of yellow flame danced from Cloudrock. I could see them licking the base of the clouds.

'What is it?' screamed Yellowbark.

The display was a deep maroon now, the sky still sucking up colours from the ground.

'Cloudrock,' I cried. 'It's gone!'

Red again. Red. Red. Red. A new shower of flames ascended. They burned out the lungs of the sky, obliterating its features.

There were still a few people on Cloudrock – had been. Now they were part of the ashes and coals that roared from the mouth of the earth below. Molten saliva splattered the rainforest, cut new grooves in the hillsides. I couldn't see it, but I knew it was happening.

'A disaster!' cried Yellowbark. 'Our *home*.'

'Gone now.'

We both fell silent and some while later a hot breath of wind from the distant furnace reached us, travelling outwards from where Cloudrock had been. There were others around us now, standing on the ridges and talking in quiet voices. Dark shapes, images of men and women, all watching the earth vomit matter from its stomach.

'Those we left behind,' I called to Yellowbark, 'are up there now, with Redgod. Part of that red glow. Each one a small cloud of sparks, cinders. Can you see the blood? If we tried very hard I think we could distinguish the blood from the red ash.'

Another blast. Another disgorgement.

'*You* did it,' she said.

I laughed.

'No one can control the earth. An *understanding*, yes . . .'

Her eyes reflected red. She was unable to comprehend. My wound was beginning to hurt and I kept my hand over it, trying to staunch the slow flow of blood.

'You'd better get me some help,' I said, 'or I'll bleed to death.'

She went.

For the next few nights we had fabulous sunsets – red, glorious red. But the clouds of ash and dust came after that, covering everything in a grey film. During the day it grew cooler and darker as clouds obscured the sun. Some of our kinfolk formed a mantle over the world.

Even when the rain came, it brought with it large gobbets of grey matter, which found its way into everything, even the food. It was impossible to keep it out. Thus, we ate the departed ones and saved their souls.

Daybreaks on the distant mountains were as crimson as sunsets. Cloudrock had become rock clouds. My homeland, blown to coke, covered the world. Every leaf, stone, tree, fish, yurt, cave, crab, monkey, ant, cat, rill, cricket, frog, person, gone. All gone. Transformed in a moment to something else. Not lost, but transformed. Part of the wind, part of the water, part of the land. Redgod revitalized. Charged with a new, tremendous influx of energy.

Some days later we continued our journey. My wound had been superficial. Once more, I led and others followed. The perfume of the distant blossoms became stronger.

Chapter Twenty-five

Well, we got here. We crossed the wastes, with its deep valleys and high cliffs; with its great skeletons of giants through which we could walk; with its fallow soils and brackish water, too bitter to hold down.

We crossed the wastes and reached fruitful country, in which we met friendly tribes and hostile peoples. We passed on, growing in numbers as others joined us in our march. There were some like Mecal, who taught us things we never dreamed. I learned to read and write, which is why you have this manuscript in your hands, absorbing my words.

We travelled a great distance – how far, none of us knows, but it is a long way from our origins. We found a land that suited us and we settled. Here we are today.

I expect you think we have changed. I suppose you believe we threw off our old ways and became like you. Well, I'm sorry to disappoint you, for if you thought that, you would be wrong.

There is still marriage within the Family. The women still eat the dead, to keep them within the cycle, the circle of blood. We still pray to our ancestors: to Redgod and the flush of twilight scarlet in the sky. The only difference now is that there is no casting out the *unwanted*. We live in mutual harmony. That's the only difference as far as I recall.

You have your religion and we have ours. You live your life the way you want to and we do the same. You'll have to be satisfied with that.

I can see one of the fires from where I sit. The sparks rise: a fine cloud of bright specks, swirling into the night, twisting turning, caught in the wind. Someone shifts a log and a fresh shower goes shooting upwards. There are people around the bonfire, talking in low voices. The sound is contentment.

Nithma is dead. She never even saw the other side of the

158

Deadlands. I don't believe she even wanted to. She was part of Cloudrock. She lost heart the day that her homeland died.

Yellowbark, that ungainly old bitch, has taken her place. She plagues me still and I dare not let the reins of power slip from my fingers, or I might see the flash of that blade again, before it buries itself in my heart. I don't want to go: not just yet. I'm enjoying myself.

I sometimes muse on what it will be like to be dead. I shall become part of my friend, the earth, then. My gases will mingle with the wind. The fluids of my body will run with the rivers. My ashes will become part of the dust. I will feed the life thereon, both plant and animal. I shall be pressed to stone. I will become the air, the ocean, the mountains. I will become the metal axe you wield, the lizard you chase from your bed, the spider that crouches by the fire. I will feed your fire as wood or coal. I will become stone in your hearth, the hawk, the fish, the berry on the bush. I will become graphite and tablet. Even you. I will become you. I have been all things and will become all things.

Too fanciful for you? Well, I was always inclined to paint with lurid colours. You will have to grit your teeth and snort at the words, if you disapprove, for I am not quite finished.

The stones are live. When I am pressed to stone, my spirit will inhabit the stone. When the rain falls and patters on the leaves of the forest, I hear my ancestors talking. When the river runs through subterranean tunnels, sounding the limestone cones, my ancestors speak with your ancestors. So it is with the wind through the spinney, or the grumbling of rocks, or the cracking of ice, the murmuring of shingle on the beach, the bark of the fox, the cry of the eagle, the snap of the beetle. All things.

Now, I've finished.

More sparks from outside.

There is a movement at my elbow. In the light of the oil lamp I see it is Clay. Since he stands directly beneath the lamp his shadow is short, while mine is long against the wall. He makes no acknowledgement of my presence, but stands there, looking thoughtfully at the words I am writing. Perhaps he disapproves of the purple, philosophical passages? No – I remember he has never learned to read and write.

I touch his hand as it rests on my writing table and he turns to stare out at the fire through the doorway. Shade, young and beautiful, is dancing there. She is shortly to be married and he will lose a daughter.

Ah, my brother, my brother. I owe you so much. I owe you my life, my liberty, and the discovery of myself. I would try to tell you, but you would not hear me. Yet you see *something* here. You see something you recognize as part of you, otherwise you would acknowledge me, speak my name, tell me your thoughts, allow me to absorb part of your unhappiness. What kind of sadness is it that makes a man turn in on himself? Do you miss her still? That much?

Lately you seem to have diminished in stature, just as I have grown. It is almost as if we were reversing roles. See! You pick up my stylus, where I have dropped it on the floor, just as I used to retrieve your arrows from the tree!

Nothing is ever destroyed. It merely changes shape. Clay is still Clay, but in a different form from that which ran through the forests of Cloudrock.

Clay has become my shadow.